PHANTOM HORSE COMES HOME

Christine Pullein-Thompson lives in a moated Rectory in Suffolk. She is married to author, Julian Popescu, and they have four children. She wrote her first book while still in her teens, and has now had more than sixty books published since then.

She began riding when she was six, and had fallen off more than a hundred times before she was twelve. At one time, she ran the Grove Riding Schools with her sisters, Josephine and twin Diana, when they had more than forty horses in their stables. She also whipped-in to the Woodland Foxhounds, competed across country, show jumped, and was a South Berkshire Gymkhana Champion. She still rides, and has three horses, a dog and a cat.

This Armada book belongs to:

Other titles by Christine Pullein-Thompson in Armada

A Day To Go Hunting
Goodbye to Hounds
Stolen Ponies
I Rode a Winner
The Horse Sale
Ride By Night

in the same series

Phantom Horse
Phantom Horse Goes to Ireland
Phantom Horse in Danger

also

Good Riding
Riding For Fun
Improve Your Riding

PHANTOM HORSE
COMES HOME

CHRISTINE PULLEIN-THOMPSON

An Armada Original

First published in the U.K. in 1970 in Armada by
Fontana Paperbacks, 14 St. James's Place, London SW1A 1PS

This impression 1980

© Christine Pullein-Thompson 1970

Printed in Great Britain by
Love & Malcomson Ltd.,
Brighton Road, Redhill, Surrey.

ILLUSTRATIONS

The author wishes to thank Les Thomson of the British Bloodstock Agency for his help with the flight of Phantom from New York to London.

Chapter One

"Come in," called Mummy opening a window. "Something has happened."

I was schooling Phantom behind Mountain Farm. It was one of those lovely spring evenings which seem as though they would last for ever. The frogs were croaking incessantly in the valley. There was an exhilarating breeze which came straight from the Blue Ridge Mountains. I had been circling, and Phantom was beginning to flex his neck and drop his jaw at last.

"What can have happened?" I wondered, riding towards the stable which our American friends called the 'barn'. My brother Angus appeared on a bicycle. He was having one of his non-riding days.

"What's happened?" he shouted.

"I don't know," I answered, untacking Phantom.

I remembered that my parents had written to various hotels about a holiday. They had been torn between Cape Cod and a holiday in Maine, which they said resembled England. We all yearned for England sometimes when the days were unbearably hot, or we were stuck in an endless jam of cars, or people laughed at us because we walked to the local drugstore.

"They must have booked a holiday," I replied walking towards the house.

"Ya, sure," replied Angus, who was beginning to talk American.

Our parents were in the sitting room. They each had a glass of sherry and Daddy was smoking a cigarette. He had just returned from Washington and was wearing an English suit. He looked tall and thin and on edge. Mummy was looking out of a window.

"Oh here you are," she said turning round.

I took off my crash cap. I felt nervous now. I wondered whether some close relation had died. There was that sort of atmosphere in the room.

"Well, what's happened?" asked Angus throwing himself into a chair.

"Someone has died. Aunt Agatha, Uncle George, Granny?" I guessed.

Time seemed to be passing very slowly until Mummy said, "You tell them," and looked at Daddy, who put his cigarette in an ashtray and straightened his tie.

"You may be pleased," he said unexpectedly. "We've got to go home."

"To England?" I asked stupidly.

"But why?" asked Angus. "I thought we were here for three years."

I thought of narrow winding lanes, of Sparrow Cottage, small and dreaming, of the paddock where our ponies had grazed beneath the tall elms. We had only been in Virginia eleven months, but already it seemed like years.

"What about school?" I asked, before I thought of Phantom and felt a lump rising in my throat. "What about Phantom?" I shouted. "I can't leave him behind."

"I don't know," replied Daddy. "I don't know why you have to collect animals wherever you go."

I think I had better explain about Phantom. He is a Palomino, golden dun with a flaxen mane and tail. He was wild in the mountains when we first came to

Virginia. He had been destined for the race track, but he had broken loose and no one had been able to catch him. Angus and I and our American friends, Phil and Pete and Wendy had tried and failed like everyone else. And whoever caught him could have him; we thought of little else during our first few weeks in Virginia. Then in the winter I had found him ill in the mountains, almost too weak to walk and had led him down from the Blue Ridge Mountains to Mountain Farm. We nursed him back to health and then slowly I had tamed him, hung sacks of hay over his back, watched him shivering with fright beneath their weight and finally backed him.

"Can't you turn him loose again?" Mummy asked. I shook my head. "He causes too much trouble. Sooner or later someone would shoot him," I replied. "When are we going anyway? He's entered for a show in May."

"In a month," Daddy replied. "The Government has fallen. There's been an election. They want me in London. I've got to brief the new man and then stay on at the Foreign Office."

"It's a step up actually," Mummy said.

"He was going in the green hunter class," I said and my voice did not sound like my own any more. "The show is on May 16th. It was to be his debut."

"That's all right then," Daddy answered. "We are going on the 19th."

"I don't know why you are so upset," Angus said. "I think it will be nice to see dear old London again."

I had forgotten what London was like. I had become geared to the American way of life. I had not wanted to leave England a year ago, and now I did not want to leave Virginia.

"We get help with travelling expenses, so we might be able to take him," Mummy said.

"You mean Phantom?" I cried.

"He would never load," Angus said. "He's too kinky. He would go berserk if he saw a ship."

"He would go by air," Daddy replied. "But are you sure he's legally yours, Jean?"

I nodded. "His owner gave me a certificate of gift. He came to see me last fall. He said I had sure earned him."

My mind was racing ahead all the time. I saw myself saying goodbye to Phil, Pete and Wendy. I might never see them again. I felt near to tears.

"I don't know why things have to change," I cried angrily.

"That's life," replied Mummy. "It wasn't meant to be a picnic."

"Supposing Phantom doesn't load?" asked Angus.

"They'll drug him," Mummy replied, "and truss him up."

I saw Phantom being drugged, myself waiting for him at London Airport, myself going back to my old school, meeting my old friends who I had said goodbye to only a year ago. Our ponies would come back, grey Moonlight and roan Mermaid. They would graze again under our elms in Oxfordshire.

"The fences won't be high enough," I said suddenly. "Phantom will jump them."

I started to bite my nails, which was something I had not done for ages. The future seemed fraught with difficulties. "I won't have any suitable tack," I said. "Everything we have here belongs to the Millers."

"We must buy some tack then," replied Daddy, sounding weary. "And build higher fences. It is lucky

I could hardly sleep that night

the cottage hasn't been let again yet. Things could be much worse. . . ."

"When shall we tell the Millers?" I asked next.

"Tomorrow we can ride over in the morning, it's Saturday," replied Angus getting out of the chair in which he had been sitting. "And for goodness sake cheer up; we are not all going to be painlessly destroyed. I'm looking forward to seeing Moonlight again, even if you don't care tuppence for Mermaid."

"Don't be so beastly, of course I care about Mermaid," I answered.

11

"But you prefer Phantom," my brother replied, leaving the room.

I could hardly sleep that night. There was bright moonlight outside, an owl hooted, and England seemed further and further away. I kept wondering whether Angus was right. Did I really like Phantom better than my thirteen-hand roan Mermaid? Then I started worrying about Phantom again—supposing all the planes were fully booked? Supposing no one could fit him in anywhere. What would I do then?

Mummy came into my room on tip-toe and drew my curtains. "Do try and sleep, Jean," she said tucking me in. "Everything will work out all right in the end."

"Are you sure?" I asked grabbing her hand.

"Certain," she replied. "Daddy will fix up everything. He will pull all the right strings, like he always does. . . ." She brushed my face with her hand and went out.

I slept and the next thing I knew was Angus shaking me, saying, "It's nearly ten o'clock, aren't you getting up at all? I've caught Phantom and Pelican."

Pelican was a wall-eyed grey lent to us by the Millers. He was a strange horse. He seemed to live removed from us all in his own private world. If you held out a titbit he just ignored it. Yet he was not blind, only wall-eyed. He never grew fat either. He was stiff and unresponsive to leg aids. He was fifteen two and sometimes we wondered how we would feel on our own much smaller ponies back in England.

Now I got out of bed and dressed in the inevitable jeans and gay checked shirt, which came from the one and only clothes shop in the nearest town. It was hot already; the frogs were croaking in the valley. The sun looked pitiless in the endless blue of the sky.

12

Phantom whinnied when he saw me. I tacked him up and we rode away across the valley towards the Millers' house, standing white and pillared in the distance.

"England is going to look awfully shut in after this," Angus said, pushing Pelican into a canter.

You could canter for ever it seemed. It made you feel like a cowboy.

"Phil and Pete won't be there," I said.

"I know," Angus answered. "But we can still tell Wendy and her parents."

We had nearly reached the house now, with its white-railed garden which the Millers called a yard. Their white-faced, red cattle were standing half in the stream shaking their heads against the flies. Their dogs sat on the lawn watching us. It seemed impossible that we were leaving, going away, never coming back. Tears blinded me for a moment; but Phantom walked on, his head high, his hoofs almost prancing over the nearly parched grass.

We found Wendy in the yard grooming her roan, Easter.

"Hi," she called. "I was just going to ride over."

"We beat you to it then," replied Angus, dismounting.

They smiled at one another and suddenly I felt shut out, unnecessary.

"We are going," Angus said. "Daddy has been recalled." He made it sound like a death knell. I dismounted and loosened Phantom's girths. I thought, soon all this will be just a memory.

"Going! Going back home? But I thought. . . ." cried Wendy.

"So did we," interrupted Angus. "But there's been an election."

"Oh heck!" shouted Wendy. "Holy cow, and we had made all sorts of plans. We had found you a place at Cape Cod for the summer." She had stopped grooming Easter. She was tall, far taller than me, with hazel eyes and red-brown hair which always seemed to stay where she wanted it. Like me, she was wearing the inevitable shirt and jeans.

"Can't you stay on here? We can put you up. There's enough room in the old place for an army," she cried. "Your father must be coming back eventually."

Angus shook his head. "We've never been posted to the same place twice. Besides he was due for a spell in England sooner or later."

"Of all the doggone luck!" exclaimed Wendy. "How about the show? You won't be gone by then, surely?"

I shook my head. "Not till the nineteenth," I replied.

"You could follow them later. Sure you could," Wendy said. "You don't have to go when they do."

"Yes we do," I replied. "And I shall be taking Phantom."

"He'll never load. You must be nuts if you think he'll load," Wendy cried. "Look at him; he's still half wild. Look at his eyes, Jean. He belongs here in the mountains."

"I'm taking him," I replied with a feeling of fury mounting inside me. "He's mine. I've got the deed of gift."

"I bet you fifty dollars he won't load," shouted Wendy.

"Done," I cried.

She looked hot and angry. She had wanted to dominate me from the moment we had met eleven months ago. Suddenly I was glad to be leaving. I looked at the dry grass, at the dust rising where some cattle were stamping under a tree, and I imagined England damp and green, small and cosy in a way America could never be. I imagined meeting friends again, drinking cider with them, sitting on the lawn at home.

"Let's ride. You girls always quarrel," said Angus in an annoying, grown-up voice.

We rode as far as the gas line and down along the rocky bed of an old stream. It was hot even for May and I kept thinking of the long hot summer which we would never see and imagining Wendy and her brothers still riding along the tracks, which Indians had used in years gone by. Mr. and Mrs. Miller were out and we parted briefly at the cattle grid which led to the stables.

"You tell your parents you gotta stay, tell them about the house at Cape Cod. Tell them you don't wanta go back to your silly little island yet. . . ." shouted Wendy. "Doggone it, you can't go. . . . We've made a lot of plans."

"England isn't a silly little island," I shouted. "It's the most civilised place in the world." But she didn't listen, only waved and rode away towards the stables looking large and American on Easter.

"Well, you did put your foot in it!" my brother exclaimed. "You said all the wrong things as usual."

"She wants her own way. She doesn't really care about us; it's *her* plans that matter." Suddenly I hated her and Angus, everybody. I pushed Phantom with my legs and we started to gallop, on and on across the

limitless landscape, and I thought, I shall make her
keep her word. I shall demand fifty dollars, and I
imagined Phantom walking behind me into a jet aircraft, the doors closing behind us, people watching,
clapping, Wendy scowling, the sun shining on the
airport, home the next stop.

Chapter Two

The next day was Sunday and we didn't go to
church. I schooled Phantom; I tried to teach him work
on two tracks but I wasn't very successful. Wendy
appeared in the afternoon.

"I've put this together for you. You'll need it for
the green hunter class." She handed me an ancient
double bridle as she dismounted from Easter. "It
hasn't a lip strap; otherwise it's okay," she added.

Angus appeared. He was nearly as tall as Wendy
and already his face was tanned by the sun.

"Have you asked about staying here?" Wendy
asked. "Just till the fall. You can stay with us. I've
fixed it."

We shook our heads. We liked the Millers but their
ways were not really our ways.

"Then we're going to visit you in the summer
vacation," cried Wendy. "We're coming over on the
new Queen. Daddy's booking right away."

I tried to imagine the Millers in England. Would
they stay with us? How would we entertain them?
And what about the food? Would they appreciate
bread and honey for tea? I fiddled with the straps of

the double bridle, while my brother said, "Sure, that's great," sounding impossibly American.

I tried to imagine them on our ponies. I could not bear to think of Wendy on Phantom. She would lose her temper with him, jerk his mouth, terrify him for ever.

"If Sparrow Cottage can't take us, we can sure stay somewhere else," replied Wendy sounding uncertain.

"Of course it will. You'll stay with us, that's settled," Angus replied.

They will bump their heads on the beams, I thought, and the spare room is tiny, and what if Mr. and Mrs. Miller want to stay as well?

I put the double bridle on Phantom, but he still didn't look like a hunter.

"I shan't win anything, he's too showy for a hunter," I said.

"Are you coming with us in the truck?" asked Wendy. "We'll have some room, because the boys won't be back home in time."

I knew their truck. It was not like a horsebox, but with rails along its sides and no top. The horse jumped into it off a loading ramp.

I shook my head. "Phantom might not load. It's only six miles. I'm hacking."

"Hacking!" shouted Wendy. "But no one hacks around here. You must be nuts."

I saw myself riding along a dirt road. "It will quieten him down for the show," I answered. "I'll allow lots of time. Mummy will bring the grooming gear in the car."

"Pete will be mad when he knows," Wendy cried. "He'll be mad at me for not stopping you."

I took the double bridle off Phantom. The day was

growing cooler now. The flies had been replaced by midges.

"He'll never get into your truck," I said. "And supposing he tried to jump over the sides? You know how wild he is. If he escaped I might never catch him again."

"Have it your own way then," replied Wendy. "But you could get a horsebox for yourself if our truck's so darned crabby."

Mummy made us tea. Wendy drank hers, with ice in it and pineapple juice, out of a tall glass with a special spoon with a long handle, which she dug out of one of the drawers in the kitchen. She ate biscuits, which she called cookies. and suddenly the sky was dark outside and everything seemed ominously still.

"There's going to be a storm," she cried. "I'm going before it starts."

Five minutes later she was galloping away across the valley and I was saying to my brother, "How are we going to put them up? Who will they ride? They are too big for Mermaid and Moonlight." And the future seemed fraught with anxiety.

"We'll fix them up somehow. We can sleep in the summer-house and they can have our rooms. Stop worrying, Jean. I'm looking forward to them coming."

"But what about horses?" I asked.

"We can take them to London, to Oxford, it will be a lovely excuse for taking them places. We needn't ride," Angus replied.

"But will our car be big enough? Supposing Daddy buys an ordinary sort of English car?" I asked.

But now the storm had broken. There were great flashes of forked lightning which lit up the whole sky and the rain fell in huge drops, soaking everything in seconds. We ran for the house, hoping that Wendy had reached home in time, and I remembered that I had never thanked her for the double bridle.

We started to tell Mummy about the Millers coming to stay and she said, "Don't let's start worrying about that yet. There's many a slip between cup and lip. We'll jump our fences when we come to them."

And I wished that I was more like her, instead of edgy and inclined to bite my nails, 'temperamental', Daddy called it.

Mummy had started packing already. There were crates in the sitting room and some of the furniture was packed in cardboard ready for the boat. I spent the evening cleaning the double bridle. Mummy and Daddy continued packing. Angus lay in the hammock on the lawn doing nothing at all for the storm had ended, and the sky was clear.

The next day Angus and I travelled with Wendy to school carrying a letter for the headmaster with us.

"It isn't fair," Angus said. "We only had four days off for Easter and we won't get four lovely months like you in the summer."

"That's just your tough luck," replied Wendy. "If you won't stay. If you must go back like kids with your parents."

I couldn't attend at school; I kept imagining myself in England again. American History seemed irrelevant now and I had done the maths before at boarding school. I drew Sparrow Cottage for Art and the teacher said that it sure looked English and wasn't it cute, and weren't there roses round the door? And then suddenly it was time to go home.

None of the trees were in blossom any more; the

whole landscape seemed to be awaiting the full fury of summer.

Mrs. Miller drove us home. "We'll sure miss you," she said. "I don't know what Wendy will do without you."

"We're like bad pennies; we'll always turn up again," replied my brother.

"But when?" asked Mrs. Miller. "We've only just got properly acquainted."

"Daddy will ask to be posted back and then we'll return by air."

"We'll keep Mountain Farm for you then," cried Mrs. Miller stopping outside our American home with a crunch of tyres.

The show was only four days away. I schooled Phantom all evening. He would lead off on either leg now, halt perfectly and rein back. I had never ridden in an American show before. Everyone will point at Phantom, I thought. They'll say, "Ain't that the horse which ran wild in the mountains all that time—Jim Morrow's horse? Doesn't he look great? Is that the little Britisher what caught him? Hasn't she got him going real good?"

And Phantom would go round the ring like a parade horse, not a hunter, but the most beautiful horse on show. And I would have done the impossible, caught the wild horse and schooled him, the horse which no one else could catch. And besides being a compliment to me it would be one for England, where I had learned everything I knew about horses.

I groomed Phantom that evening until his tail was like cream silk, and his coat gleamed like gold. I oiled his elegant two-coloured hoofs and I imagined myself riding him down the lane to Sparrow Cottage, and I

Phantom started to trot

suddenly felt happier than I had ever felt before.

The day of the show dawned fine. Angus was not taking Pelican, but he didn't seem to mind.

"I'm not a competing person," he said. "And what would Pelican win anyway with his wall eye and inflexible neck?"

Wendy was riding her father's horse, a big grey called Seashore.

The day was hot from the start and I knew that by lunch-time every living thing would be stationary in the valley, cows standing under trees, or in the stream, people in deck chairs or hammocks, or working inside barns and houses. No one, but the competitors at the horse show would be riding by lunch-time.

I had cleaned my riding clothes the evening before. I had nearly outgrown my jodhpurs, my boots pinched my toes, my hacking jacket was too short, but at least I had a hunting whip and, thanks to Wendy, the right bridle.

Phantom was still clean. I tacked him up and Mummy said, "Are you sure you are all right? Don't do anything silly."

Daddy had taken the car to Washington. Mummy and Angus were to come later to the show with the Millers.

I pulled up my girths and mounted. My tummy had started to flutter. "It's straight all the way. I shall be all right. Don't worry," I replied, straightening my crash cap.

"Touch wood," shouted Angus.

I picked up the double reins, slid my little fingers between them. I felt like a million dollars now and I was still happy with the sort of happiness which seems indestructible, but which is really as fragile as glass.

I waved as I rode out of the gate. Phantom walked with a long stride, his head high, his ears pricked. I leaned forward to pat his neck. I wanted to shout, "All my dreams have come true." Instead, I rode past rail fences onto a dirt road and straightaway Phantom started to trot, his neck arched, his hoofs hardly seeming to touch the ground.

We must have trotted for a mile or more when I had the feeling that Phantom had been the same way before, many, many times, perhaps by moonlight when he was wild, enticing mares from their fields to keep him company in the mountains. I made him walk as a Cadillac hurtled by leaving a trail of dust behind it. I felt him quiver and suddenly I thought, perhaps he's never been ridden on a road before. I turned him onto the verge and we trotted and I watched the lather growing under his bridle and his ears grow dark with sweat and I thought, I hope Mummy remembers the grooming things, otherwise he'll look awful for the hunter class.

The day was growing hotter now. There wasn't a cloud in the sky. I passed a wooden house. A negro lay outside, swinging in a hammock hung from a mulberry tree and I thought, England will seem kind of foreign after this. There were high rail fences on each side of us now and in the distance stables and behind us the negro had started to sing, and his deep throaty voice seemed to belong to the countryside. I could hear a truck coming now, its engine drowning his voice and even then I had no sense of impending disaster. It came nearer and I felt Phantom brace himself. I shortened my reins. "It's nothing, just a truck," I told him.

He started to jump in the air and the driver shouted, "Hi there! Get off the road. This ain't no place for horses, no siree." He stopped the truck as Phantom went up on his hind legs. I leaned forward, grabbing his mane. I was afraid I would pull him over on top of me, but he came down again on the grass verge. I could smell petrol fumes and the driver was still shouting. Then without warning I was on the bank at the side of the road and I knew with awful certainty that Phantom was going to jump the rails.

They looked enormous, higher than anything I had ever jumped before and I had lost my stirrups now. He took off and I hit my face on his neck and I could taste blood on my lips. Then he was over and I was hurtling towards the ground and all my hopes had gone.

I landed on my shoulder. As I scrambled to my feet I saw him galloping away in the distance. He cleared another fence, taking it in his stride, and I thought, he's going back to the Blue Ridge Mountains, I shall never have him now, and a great wave of desolation swept over me. The truck had disappeared and I remembered Angus shouting "Touch wood", and I hadn't touched it. I was filled with superstition and regret.

I imagined Daddy cancelling the booking for Phantom, the collecting ring steward at the show calling my name over and over again, men in white Panama hats turning to say to one another, "I knew she would never make it. A girl is no match for that horse, no siree. . . ."

My eyes were pricking with tears now. The heat was unbearable, the fields seemed endless and the Blue Ridge Mountains never seemed to grow any nearer. My jodhpur boots were pinching my toes, so I took them off and walked barefoot, keeping my eyes open for vipers and snakes.

The sun grew hotter and, as I climbed a wall, I wondered whether Mummy had left for the show yet and what she would say when she found I had never arrived. Would she and Mrs. Miller look for me along the dirt road? I turned back towards the road, because I didn't want to walk for ever round and round in circles, climbing fence after fence and never getting any nearer home. It was even hotter on the road; nothing seemed to move besides myself and small black pebbles got between my toes, so that in the end I was forced to put my boots on once more. And now I was hating the very size of America. I was thinking, in England someone would have picked me up hours ago, the truck driver would have stopped, he would have helped me pursue Phantom. . . . And then a truck did slow down and a voice called, "Hi there, do you want a lift? Hop in," and a young man stopped beside me holding open the cab door.

I climbed up gratefully. "I'm not supposed to take lifts actually," I said.

"Where do you come from? You don't come from here, I know that," he said leaning across me to shut the door.

"England," I replied.

"And you've lost your horse," he said. "That's kinda tough. Are you all right, no cuts or anything? Did you hit your head?"

"No, I'm fine thanks," I answered.

He was young with fair hair and a white shirt and jeans and he drove his truck barefoot. We talked about England, and he said he wanted to taste our fish and chips and I said, "They're ghastly really, and you have to eat them in newspaper if you want to eat them properly." And all the time I could feel my spirits sinking lower and lower and it was as though someone else was talking, not me at all.

"They sure sound fine anyway," he said agreeably.

We were nearly home now and I kept remembering how gleefully I had started out without a trace of anxiety in my mind. I scanned the Blue Ridge Mountains for a galloping horse but there was nothing to be seen besides the trees reaching upwards towards the sky.

"This is where I live," I cried, pointing to Mountain Farm. "Thanks a million for the lift."

"That's okay, any time," he said. "I sure hope you find your horse."

"I won't," I answered with a choke in my voice. "I don't suppose I shall ever see him again."

He opened the cab door and I stepped out into the heat of midday. My shirt was sticking to my back. My toes felt raw in my boots. He waved and smiled and waved again and shouted, "I'll be seeing you." And as he drove away I thought, that was one lift which was all right anyway. I walked towards the house and, as I walked, I could feel the tears coming, first as a trickle and then as a flood and suddenly I was running, shouting, "Mummy, are you home? I've lost Phantom. He's gone back to the mountains. I've lost him for ever." I wiped my face with the back of my hand mixing dust with the tears and I thought, I never want to see the Millers again. I wish we were leaving tomorrow and then I remembered the double bridle and I imagined Phantom hung up somewhere by the reins, struggling till his mouth bled, and everything had the quality of a nightmare, only I knew I wouldn't wake up, it would be there for ever.

I imagined the house empty before I reached it, the blinds pulled down in the sitting room, the large grandfather clock noisily giving time away in the hall. Time! I thought. It must be two o'clock, time for the green hunter class. . . . I shall never ride in an American show now, never, and my tears fell unchecked like falling rain on the short paved path. And then I heard Mummy calling from the yard at the back.

"Jean, where are you? We've got him, we've got

Phantom." And my brother came tearing round the corner of the house and stopped dead in his tracks. "So you've got here," he cried. "I was just going to organise a search party."

I ran round to the stable. Phantom was standing in his box still blowing, his sides dark with sweat.

"We couldn't believe it when we heard hoofs. He came over the gate. It must be five foot. Are you all right, Jean?" Mummy asked.

"He came home. He didn't go back to the mountains. He didn't want to," I shouted, and for a moment nothing else mattered.

Mummy had loosened his girths. Gradually his sides stopped going in and out like bellows. He raised his head and looked at me and I said, "Thank you for coming back," and then, "What's the time? Can I still get there in time?"

"It's just gone one," Angus replied, looking at his watch. "You might make it yet. I'll tack up Pelican and come with you. I'll ride on the outside, between you and the traffic."

"I'll get him ready while you change," I cried, running up the stirrups on Phantom's saddle, for miraculously they were still there. I put the reins under them and ran for Pelican's pelham and saddle while Mummy stood by saying, "You're horse mad, both of you. Do be careful. I can't stand much more."

"I'll keep between you and the traffic," Angus repeated a moment later mounting Pelican. "You must enter. It's your last chance."

"I wish I could follow you in the car," Mummy said. "Are your girths tight? Put the elastic under your chins."

"We'll be all right," I yelled.

27

We were riding away now. "Thanks a million," I said, smiling at Angus. "I thought I was never going to see Phantom again."

Angus looked small on Pelican. He rode in one hand. We cantered along a wide grass verge and people leaned out of cars to look at us.

"They think we're mad riding along a road," Angus said. "I suppose horses always go by box or truck here."

"It's like walking," I replied. "Only nut cases walk."

"He must like us to come back," Angus said looking at Phantom.

"I know. It was almost worth falling off to know that," I replied.

We clattered through a village which consisted only of a few houses and a drug store. People ran to gates and windows to watch us.

"Look," shouted Angus. "There's the show. Look, over there." He stood in his stirrups and pointed and I could see a ring fenced by a wooden rail fence. People were riding round it in groups.

"It must be the family class," shouted Angus. "Was it before the green hunters?"

I couldn't remember and I realised with dismay that I had left my schedule on my dressing table at home. I had plaited Phantom in the morning and three of his plaits had come undone. His bridle was filthy, his sides coated with dust. There wasn't a trace of hoof oil left on his hoofs.

"We had better walk," I said. "Phantom's soaked in sweat. Can you lend me a handkerchief? My face feels filthy."

I could hear the faint sound of music and wondered whether Pete and Phil had arrived home yet from their

28

military academy. There were hundreds of cars parked by the ringside and now we could hear an announcer calling out numbers. There were flags round the outside course hanging limply on their poles, and children looking like ants scuttling about with numbers tied to their backs. I felt unbearably tense now. There was a strange flutter in my tummy, and my legs felt like jelly. I spat on Angus's handkerchief and rubbed my face. Phantom stopped to gaze at the scene below. He arched his neck and pranced.

"He looks like a million dollars. He must win a prize. Come on, let's hurry," cried Angus.

The scene below grew larger; the ants became children. I could see the outside course properly now, high and solid. Phantom danced into the show ground and I saw Mummy waving and shouting, "I've got your number. Your class is in Ring Two. They're halfway through."

Pete was waving too. "They've been calling for you," he shouted.

"Holy cow! What happened to you?" asked Wendy, appearing on Seashore, who looked marvellous, his mane braided, his hoofs oiled.

"I can't go in like this," I said, halting Phantom. "Look at his mane and hoofs. He's filthy."

"I've brought some rubber bands," cried Mummy, delving in her pockets. "I'll fix his mane."

"Doggone it, where's some hoof oil?" shouted Pete.

"I'll get a rubber," yelled Angus.

Someone was tying a number to my back. The band was playing a march. Angus was rubbing saddle soap into Phantom's bridle while he stood like a statue, sniffing the air.

"They are calling you again, you had better go,"
said Mummy.

Chapter Three

I rode down a sloping field past a party taking
bottles of Californian wine from an estate waggon.
Phantom started to prance and I heard a man say,
"Sure that's the wild horse. I would know him anywhere, and that's the little English girl who found
him in the mountains dying. She's got nerve, that girl,
yes siree."

Pete caught me up. He had changed out of his
uniform into trousers and a nylon shirt. "Gee, Phantom
looks good," he exclaimed. "Keep your nerve. You're
doing all right."

He had grown some more. He must have been five
foot ten; but Phil was taller still, six foot plus and
still growing. Pete had fair hair and brown eyes and
his nose wasn't quite straight. Phil was as handsome
as a film star, with dark hair and a long, lean body.
All the girls turned to look at him as he passed. But
I preferred Pete, who was less spoilt and kinder.

I could feel my heart beating against my side like
a sledge hammer as I reached the ring.

"So you've shown up at last," said the collecting
ring steward. "I sure hope the judge will have you
now."

The band was still playing the same march. It made
me think of musical poles at home, of cantering round
and round the damp green English turf on Mermaid,

while the riders and the poles grew fewer and my friends yelled, "Gallop, Jean. Look, over there!" Suddenly I felt a long way from home and more alien than I had ever felt before. Phantom started to snort and the steward said, "Okay. You can go in now."

The green hunters were lined up in the centre of the ring. A judge was looking at their legs.

"Good luck," shouted Angus, his voice sounding very English amid a babble of American voices.

"Walk on," I told Phantom.

This was my great moment for which I had worked for months, to show everyone that I had tamed the wild horse of the Blue Ridge Mountains; but now Phantom wasn't going. He was running backwards, gazing at the ring with frightened eyes.

"He thinks it's a corral," I shouted to Pete. "Can you lead him?"

"I'll try."

But he was on his hind legs now. A second later he came down again with a piercing snort, which made the horses in the ring raise their heads in alarm. His tail was kinked over his back and he started to do a sort of high school dance.

I leaned down and stroked his neck. "It's all right, Phantom. It isn't a trap," I said, and could feel him relaxing as I spoke, and I thought, everything's going to be all right; he's going in. Then from somewhere behind me I heard a man say, "Hi, you over there, give me my whip. That's no horse for a girl. He needs a man to master him." There was no time for the words to sink in. For a brief second I was speechless and then as I collected my wits the whip caught Phantom round his hind legs. He leapt forward twenty feet or more, and now we were galloping and I couldn't stop him, nothing on earth could stop him. It was like running away on an express train. Picnickers scattered; children ran; there was a tumult of shouting from behind and nothing in front but fields and the Blue Ridge Mountains in the distance waiting to wrap us in their silence and calm. And I knew how he felt . . . he could trust those mountains, they were like the four walls of home to him. I pulled on the reins without avail. He cleared a wall without pausing, his tail streaming behind him like a flag and I wondered what Mummy was thinking, what the crowds were saying now, and how long it would take to school Phantom to enter a ring and not turn wild at the first touch of the whip.

And all the time that I was wrenching and pulling on the reins I wasn't really frightened, for I knew he would stop in the end, that I would get off him then and lead him home. But I shall never be able to ride him properly in an American show now, I thought, and they'll go on hatching libellous stories about him long after I've returned to England. The mountains were looming larger now. I could see the trees on them; they were no longer just a blue smudge in the distance.

I don't know how many more fences we cleared. I sat still, a passenger on the fastest little horse in Virginia. And then at last I saw the roof of Mountain Farm and I thought, he's going home again. He really does like living with us. I hope he likes Sparrow Cottage as much; at least Englishmen keep their whips to themselves.

I could see a car parked in the yard and people waving. The sweat from Phantom's sides stung my legs through my jodhpurs. All my strength seemed gone. Phantom broke into a trot when he reached the yard. He raised his head and neighed for Pelican and it was like a trumpet call from a returning warrior. I slid to the ground. My legs almost buckled under me. It was the Millers' car I had seen. They came racing round the corner of the house. Mrs. Miller had her hair, which was so like Wendy's, piled on the top of her head. She wore a canvas skirt and canvas shoes and a blue silk blouse.

"Heavenly day!" she cried. "Are you all right, Jean? We thought he was heading straight for the mountains."

Mummy was there too, looking small and frightened in a denim skirt, shirt and sneakers, and Pete was smiling, his broad, kind smile. Mr. Miller stood behind them all looking round and cuddly like a huge brown bear. "That horse will never go in a ring. He'll always be wild. You can't teach an old horse new tricks," he said.

"He isn't old," I cried. "He's only six. I shall ride him in English shows."

"I bet you five hundred dollars he won't go in another darned ring all his life," shouted Mr. Miller.

From far away I heard my own voice shout, "Done," and Mr. Miller's reply, "Of all the doggone people. She's sure got courage, yes siree."

And I shouted back, as I walked limping to the stable, "I've already got a bet with Wendy about the aeroplane, she thinks I'll never get him in."

Pete helped me take the tack off. "I sure hope you don't lose. Have you really got all that money, Jean?" he asked. "The old man likes his debts paid."

33

"Sure," I replied with a shivery feeling down the back of my spine.

"I'll pay if you like," Pete answered.

"Pay?" I cried. "I'm not going to be the one who pays. I'm going to win."

"You thought that this afternoon," answered Pete. "I'll carry the saddle. You look kind of tired."

I took off my jodhpur boots and walked to the house barefoot.

"You looked like someone from another world flying across the landscape just now," Mummy said. "Were you terrified?"

"Not really," I answered. "But why did that man hit Phantom? We would have been all right otherwise. He was going to go in. He was, honestly. I could feel it."

I saw Mr. Miller laughing with disbelief and suddenly I hated him. "Where's Angus?" I asked. "What's the time? I'm starving."

"About four o'clock," I expect," Mummy replied. "Angus is waiting at the show with Pelican. The Millers are bringing them both home in the truck."

"I'd better be going," Pete said. "The old man's waiting. Be seeing you, Jean."

I watched him go, kind, broad-shouldered Pete, across the dusty yard. Mrs. Miller was hooting the Buick's horn.

"They are very kind. They brought me here at once, even though Wendy was just about to ride," Mummy said.

"I would like to kill the man who hit Phantom," I cried. "I would really. Why did he do it? It was none of his business."

"You'll never have the chance to do anything,"

Mummy answered, putting the kettle on. "Daddy rang through from Washington. Phantom's flying from Kennedy Airport, New York, in three days time."

"Why New York?" I asked. "Am I going with him?" Suddenly everything was moving too fast. It was as though life had been speeded up by an invisible switch almost to breaking point.

"That's the trouble," Mummy replied. "They want a groom, someone older than you, who is used to flying with horses."

"But Phantom won't know him. He hates strangers. He won't load and supposing he goes mad on the 'plane? He knows me, can't you see that?" I cried.

"Daddy will be home quite soon. You can talk to him," replied Mummy wearily. "I've had enough for one day."

I wandered outside and could hear the sound of crickets already, though dusk had yet to come. The air was completely still. The heat of the sun was cooling at last. Already I was privately saying goodbye to everything. I thought, if I can't fly with Phantom, perhaps I should leave him behind in the valley he loves. And then I imagined him being chased again through the Blue Ridge Mountains, facing another winter alone with the tracks deep in snow, with icicles hanging from the trees snapped in half by hurricanes. I imagined him bitten by a rabied fox, dying slowly while the buzzards ate his flesh and the flies besieged his eyes. I imagined him alone for months on end, lonely and deserted. I imagined him coming down to Mountain Farm in search of me and I would be gone. Then I heard a hoot and saw that Daddy was waiting for me to open the yard gate.

"Did Phantom go all right? Did you have any luck?" he called.

I shook my head. "Everything went wrong," I yelled. "Angus isn't home yet."

Daddy left the car in front of the house. It was covered with fine dust.

"I've booked the flight. You've got to fly from New York. He's going in a Boeing, flying through the night. It was the best I could do," he told me. He looked tall and apologetic, slim and cosmopolitan.

"I've got to go with him," I said in a tight voice. "I can't just hand him over to someone. He hates Americans. He was brought up by an English groom. It was when he died that Phantom ran away. Something awful must have happened in between."

"It's a nice story, particularly if you're English," replied Daddy. "But are you sure it's true?"

I nodded. "It was an American who upset everything today. He doesn't like Pete near him either and no one could be nicer with horses than he."

"They may be able to find an English groom. I did mention you. I may be able to pull strings. But it's all very difficult," replied Daddy, going indoors and shutting the door after him, while I stood listening to a truck coming along the road, rattling in the way the Millers' truck rattled.

I opened the gate. Angus waved. He was holding Pelican and the horses looked sweet standing and looking over the sides. There was a loading ramp at the side of the yard and when we let the back down Pelican jumped on to it without any fuss.

"It's real nice to think you're still alive," Wendy said smiling at me.

"Thanks a million," I replied.

"I jumped Pelican round the outsize course. He went like a bomb," Angus told me. "So nobody can call him a useless old nag ever again."

Wendy waved as the truck left the yard. "Be seeing you. We'll call you up," she shouted.

Angus had his arm round Pelican and suddenly I wished we could take him too. Life seemed unfair. I had Phantom, but Angus only had Moonlight who was thirteen two and much too small.

We turned Pelican into the field with Phantom. We watched them roll and the sun was setting. "There's only three more days," I said.

"I know," replied Angus. "And England is going to feel awfully shut in after here."

"We'll get used to it," I replied.

"Dinner," Mummy called, opening a window. "Hurry. We are going out."

"What, all of us?" Angus asked.

"No, just Daddy and I. We've got to say goodbye to some people. Someone's got up a party for us. We've got to go to Washington," replied Mummy, shutting the window.

"But what about us?" Angus asked when we were indoors.

"You'll be all right. You are quite old after all."

"And there's the telephone," I said. "Can you leave us a number?"

"Yes, of course, darling," Mummy replied in an absent-minded way. I don't want to go really; but it's too late to refuse now."

There was chicken and sweet corn for dinner, and a lemon meringue pie. Afterwards Mummy put on a long dress and earrings and gold sandals and Daddy put on a dinner jacket. Angus and I stood around looking envious.

"Go to bed and don't worry, oh and here's the telephone number," Mummy said, giving me a scrap of paper. "If you feel lonely, ring the Millers and have a chat."

"And lock up after us," Daddy told us. "And keep the door locked. We're taking the back door key."

"We'll watch telly," Angus replied. "Have a lovely time."

The moon had risen. It always seemed larger than an English moon, but then everything in the States seemed larger; it was just the vastness of the distances, the miles and miles between horizons.

We listened to the car starting up. "Come on, now, for telly," Angus said.

We sat and watched, one programme followed another and we could not bear the thought of bed. "Supposing they crash on the way home?" I asked Angus. "What will happen to us?"

"Why should they?" he replied.

"I feel all creepy," I said a moment later.

"Let's go to bed," suggested Angus, but now we did not feel brave enough.

"I'm sure I can hear footsteps," I said presently. "Listen!"

"You are so nervy," grumbled Angus, but I saw that he had turned pale. "It's only just eleven."

"I can hear a truck," I said. "It's stopped in the yard.

"You're mad," my brother cried. "What's there to be afraid of anyway?"

"It's someone stealing Phantom," I cried. "They

must have seen him at the show. We must do something."

I wished I was braver. I was shaking as though I had a fever and my teeth had started to chatter, and fear is infectious. In a few minutes Angus had it too.

"I'll get a knife," he said going into the kitchen. And then his voice came back quite unlike his usual voice. "You are right; there is a truck in the yard. It's got the headlights on."

"It must be all right then. I don't know why we are frightened," I said. "Thieves wouldn't have their lights on."

We looked out of a window. There were three men and one of them was a negro with only one leg.

"I'll check the doors and windows just to be on the safe side," Angus said, brandishing the carving knife.

I remembered things I had read in the papers—murders, beatings, people being tied up, their mouths sealed by tape.

Then we heard a banging on the door and a voice called, "Open up. We need a light."

"They're lying," Angus said. "It's a trick."

"Hi there, what's the matter? Are you on your own?" called another voice.

And I, like a fool, yelled, "Yes," and Angus kicked me and shouted, "No," muttering, "Fool," to me at the same time.

We went upstairs and opened a window and looked out. The moon was obscured by clouds but we could make out the three men and one of them shouted, "We've got a flat. Have you got a flashlight?"

Angus found a torch and threw it out of a window. The negro caught it and we watched them crossing the yard and I started to wonder why we had been so frightened.

"They look a rough lot," Angus said, "Rough enough for anything."

"The negro is like Long John Silver," I replied, "in *Treasure Island.*" We went back to the telly, but we couldn't concentrate any more.

I thought how peaceful it would be in England, how the people would talk like us and we would understand them and then the men came back and one of them shouted, "Hi there. We've put the light in the porch," and presently we heard their engine start.

"We won't tell the Millers about it," said Angus with a sheepish grin.

"No siree. It was because we're tired," I said. "Normally we couldn't have been scared."

"Normally Mummy and Daddy would be here," replied Angus.

The clock in the hall struck midnight. We could hear the frogs croaking in the valley as we dragged our weary legs upstairs to bed.

"Only two more days," said Angus.

"Yeah," I answered, too tired suddenly to worry any more.

Chapter Four

I fell asleep as soon as my head touched the pillow. The next thing I knew was Mummy standing beside my bed, while the first rosy light of dawn pierced the curtains. She was still in her evening dress, but she had taken off her shoes. For a moment I thought I was dreaming.

"You are awake then?" she asked.

"Sort of . . ." I answered, rubbing sleep from my eyes. "Was the party all right? Some men came in a truck." I was still half under the bedclothes.

"The gate into the road was open," Mummy said. "The horses seem to have gone. There are tyre marks all across the field to the yard gate."

I was sitting up now. "Oh no!" I cried. "You mean Phantom's gone?"

Suddenly Daddy was there too, still in his dinner jacket. "I'm afraid so, Jean," he said. "We've been on to the State police already, so don't panic."

"There were some men in a truck," I repeated. "They must have come by the field."

The gate from the field led on to the highway.

"You may as well cancel Phantom's booking," I said. "We'll never see him again now, not alive. It just isn't possible. It's fate," I added. "It's been against me ever since we were ordered home. What an awful end to an awful day." I was choking back tears now.

"It isn't the end of a day, it's a new day," cried Mummy drawing back my curtains. "Look, the sun is rising."

"I don't care about the sun," I cried leaping out of bed.

Angus had appeared now in a dressing gown. He must have heard us talking for he asked, "How did they get out?"

"The men in the truck must have come across the field," I shouted. "Don't ask me why. I knew they were a disaster. Why didn't we think of looking at the gates?" I was pulling clothes over my pyjamas now—jeans and a pullover—I imagined Phantom colliding with a truck on the highway. "Pelican must have led the way out," I cried. "Phantom liked it here. He was happy. He could have jumped the fence any time, but he didn't want to."

I rushed to the window and looked out. The valley was bathed in the rosy light of dawn. The moon was still in the sky, pale and soft, like something old and faded. Nothing moved outside, even the frogs had stopped croaking and the flies hadn't yet risen from the brambles. I could see cattle lying down near the stream.

He's gone, I thought. I shall never see him again. I always knew having him was too good to be true. Horses like him don't exist to be ridden like other horses. It was a fantasy that couldn't last. There seemed no point in searching the valley. We had no horses to scour the mountains; it was too early to telephone the Millers for help and Daddy had contacted the State police. I felt inadequate and useless. Mummy had made some tea out of tea bags. We drank it in the kitchen. "He'll come back," she said. "After all he came back twice yesterday."

"They may have gone to the Millers," Angus suggested. "It's Pelican's home."

"Sometimes I wish you had never learned to ride," said Daddy. "I have to be in Washington tomorrow at eleven. I mean *this* morning. I think I'm going to bed."

At that moment the telephone rang. "I'll get it," shouted Angus. "Somebody must have found them." As he disappeared towards the telephone I wondered why he was so optimistic.

"Perhaps it's the Millers," Mummy said. "They may have been woken by hoof beats."

We could hear Angus talking. He seemed to be taking down an address. Suddenly I was too frightened to listen. I had a terrifying sense of impending tragedy. I walked up and down the kitchen biting my nails.

"They seem to be on a highway," remarked Daddy, who had changed into pyjamas.

"Oh God!" I said. "Anything but that."

Then Angus returned to the kitchen looking very pale. "There's a dead horse on Highway Thirteen. It's grey. It could be Pelican," he said in a dull voice. Suddenly he seemed very small. "What are we going to do?" he asked. "Pelican isn't even ours; he's the Millers'."

"What did the police say?" asked Daddy.

"They want us to identify him," replied Angus with a choke in his voice. "He's on the verge."

There was a short silence before Daddy said, "I had better change," and his voice sounded incredibly weary and I thought, he's got to be in Washington at eleven. He won't get any sleep.

Angus and I found shoes. We didn't speak, for suddenly there seemed nothing left to say.

Mummy changed out of her evening dress into slacks and a polo-necked jumper. There were dark shadows under her eyes. Morning had come now, a bright summer morning. We all climbed into the car. The yard gate was open. Angus passed Daddy a scrap of paper.

"That's the location," he said, "as given me by the State cops." He sounded older and sadder and wiser.

I wondered what the Millers would say when they

heard that Pelican was dead. They might not make a fuss, they might just say, "He was an old nag anyway. We never rode him till you came. He just stayed out with the work horses doing nothing," or they might start ranting and raving and calling us "Blah blah English, who couldn't keep gates shut", for they were as unpredictable as English weather.

There was a speed limit on the highway. Daddy drove cautiously and presently we saw a car and cops standing in the highway and drew into the side. One of the cops called, "Are you the owners? He's over there."

Angus was crying now and so was I. I covered my face with my hands and started to get out of the car, and all the time I was thinking, it may be Phantom because he does look grey in the moonlight, like a phantom, and I was remembering the first time I had seen him galloping free and wild across the valley. and how I had wanted him and sought him since that moment almost to the point of madness.

"I'll go first," said Daddy looking at me. "You stay here. Tell me how I can identify him."

"He had shoes. He was flea-bitten. He had a wall eye," Angus answered.

"He's golden," I said. "With . . ." I couldn't say any more. I felt as though I was suffocating, choking to death.

"I'll come with you," Mummy said.

"We're cowards," Angus told me. "Why don't we go?"

I couldn't answer. Tears were running like a river down my face. Then Daddy came back. The State cops called, "Good morning, sir." They were big burly men with revolvers in their belts. Daddy started

44

the engine. "It hadn't any shoes," he said. "It was a dark grey and quite young I should think."

"Poor thing," I said, but I didn't stop crying, everything seemed sad now, life, the morning, the fact that we were going to England, the poor dead horse.

"We had better go home and sleep," said Mummy. "We're all at breaking point."

It was six o'clock now; the valley was coming to life. We could hear a negro singing on his way to work.

Daddy parked the car outside the house. "God, what a night!" he exclaimed.

We went into the house and Mummy made toast and bacon and eggs. Then we returned to bed and slept the dreamless sleep of complete exhaustion.

.   .   .   .   .   .

When I wakened Daddy had already left for Washington. Mummy was preparing lunch. There was the steady buzz of traffic on the highway and I could hear Angus talking on the telephone.

"The Millers haven't seen them," he said coming into my room a moment later. "But they are coming straight over."

"You might have waited before you telephoned," I replied. "What's the time?"

"One o'clock." My legs were stiff when I jumped out of bed and my head ached. I dressed and walked slowly downstairs.

"You look awful," Mummy greeted me. "Do sit down. There's only a cold lunch. Angus has been on to the Millers."

"Yes, I know. I sat on a chair and stared out of the

45

window at the stable where Phantom had been only yesterday, which now seemed a million years ago. If only we could put the clock back, I thought. If only we had gone out and helped the men with the truck we might have noticed the gate was open; but we were too feeble, too scared. How I hate myself.

"Come on, lunch," Mummy said. "Sit down. Where's Angus?"

"I've just been on to the State cops again," Angus said appearing. "They've got nothing to report. We've got two days, Jean, so do cheer up. We'll find them yet."

"With broken legs," I answered, "on Highway Thirteen."

"If they were still on the highway the police would know," Mummy replied. "Don't be an idiot, Jean."

"I wish we weren't going home," I answered. "There would be some hope then."

"We'll look for them this afternoon. We can walk," my brother replied.

And then we heard hoofs coming across the yard outside. We rushed to the window. Pete and Wendy had arrived, riding Frances and the bay mare.

"Hi," shouted Wendy, "what're you doing?"
They dismounted as we joined them outside, their faces red from riding.

"Tough luck about your horses going," Pete said.

Frances was rubbing her skewbald head on my shirt. I remembered the hours I had spent on her back in the past. We had shared a great deal together, good and bad.

"We reckoned you could do with these," Pete told us, tall and sun-tanned, his shoulders slouched.

46

"We've gotta go to Washington, but we'll be back later."

"Here's Mummy," cried Wendy. "Take the horses. We gotta go real fast. She didn't want us to come in the first place."

They were running across the yard now. We held their horses, shouting, "Thank you," wondering how we could ever repay them for their generosity.

"Some friends," muttered Angus.

"They could have cursed us for losing Pelican," I answered.

They were waving out of the station waggon's windows, yelling, "Be seeing you." And I wondered where we would find such friends again.

Mrs. Miller's face was set and angry. "You do that again," she shouted. "You darned rebels . . ."

Angus was patting the bay mare, who had never had a name. She was wiry and quick, a real cow pony people said, while Frances was a proper apache with a long head and a canter which seemed to last for ever.

"We may as well start looking straight away," Angus said. "Here, hold the bay mare while I get the headcollars."

The day was hot now. The ponies hung their heads. There will be a breeze in the mountains, I thought, there always is.

"Shall we separate?" asked Angus, swinging on to his saddle. "They can't have got to the mountains without jumping half a dozen fences which Pelican could never manage."

"I'll go to the right then," I answered, turning Frances with one hand. "Be seeing you."

Our horses parted without argument. The sun was

in my eyes. "See you in about an hour," shouted Angus.

I saw Mummy waving. She shouted something which I didn't hear. There were white shacks in the distance along the highway, and a line of electric cables and a 'plane crossing the blue sky as lonely as a solitary bird. And gradually, as I rode, I could feel hope coming back. Two days seemed a long time when I divided it into hours. Anything could happen in that time. I started to sing as I cantered, my eyes searching for horses, my mind planning the future.

Chapter Five

I kept within sight of the highway and to the right of the mountains. Angus was riding towards a town called Middlesburg. The 'plane had disappeared across the horizon. I saw some wild turkeys, longer legged than the English turkeys. A man was crossing a distant field astride a tractor. Cars passed incessantly along the highway, large and opulent, gleaming chromium and window shine. There were boulders scattered on the ground. The night seemed to have belonged to another time and place. My feeling of panic had gone. I felt one with Frances, welded to her in the way a horseman feels who has spent half his life on a horse. I belonged to the countryside too as the cars never could.

After ten minutes or more I drew rein and scanned the horizon. Frances dropped her head, stretching her

I drew rein and scanned the horizon

neck and blowing. I couldn't see my brother any more. I pushed Frances into a canter again. The sun was full in my eyes now and, as the day grew hotter, I started to long for rain, for the soft English drizzle which falls so often at home. And then Frances stopped. She raised her head and neighed and from somewhere quite near an answering neigh came back. I wanted to cheer then and I wished that Angus was with me as I pushed Frances forward, leaving the reins loose on her neck, and already I was seeing myself leading Phantom home, while Pelican followed across the sun-drenched valley to Mountain Farm. I unwound the headcollar from around my neck while Frances trotted joyfully towards some boulders where I found Phantom. He was half on the ground, his coat dark with sweat, his forelegs caught to the elbow in a tangle of barbed wire. Beside him ran a stone wall which he must have jumped without seeing the pile of rusting wire on the landing side. I thought, tetanus! He'll get it, as I leapt on to the ground and he raised his head and nickered as though he had known all along that I would come in the end. I knelt beside him talking. "It's all right," I said, stroking his wet neck. "I'll get you free. Stay still, don't worry." And all the time I was forcing back the tears which were threatening to choke me. He rubbed his head on my shoulder and tried to stand; and I saw the blood on his legs and the flies feeding on it as he sank back again on to the dusty, churned-up earth. I pulled at the wire. In places it was buried in weeds and part of it was stuck under one of his shoes. I stood up and saw that Pelican was grazing peacefully on the other side of the wall and that less than half a mile away the highway wound its way to Washington. I shall need wire cutters, I thought, and the vet and an anti-tetanus injection, and even that may be too late. I didn't feel like crying now, only suddenly resolute and determined. "I'll be back," I said, standing up. "Stay still. I'm going to get you free." Then I was vaulting on to Frances, galloping as though my life depended on it towards the Millers' house in the distance. Time passed slowly. It was ages before the house grew any nearer, and now the terrors of the night and early morning had returned. I saw Phantom dying of tetanus, the vet saying, "There's no hope. I'll get the humane killer from my automobile," myself leaving for home without him.

There was no one in the Millers yard when I reached it. I rushed to the house and Annie, the negro help, found me wire cutters. "You look real terrible!" she exclaimed. "What has happened?"

"I can't explain, but Phantom's hurt," I replied and she understood.

"The horse that lived in the mountains, sure I know him," she said.

I had left Frances tied to the yard gate. She was still blowing as I vaulted on to her back again. She did not want to go now, and though I could understand her feelings I hit her with the ends of the reins and somehow we crossed the valley again, jumping the stream, avoiding the boulders by a miracle. Phantom seemed hardly to have moved but his legs had fresh blood on them. I worked frantically with the wire cutters and, because I hurried, I kept cutting unnecessary strands. Once Phantom tried to get up, pulling the strands tighter against his legs so that the barbs sank deeper into his flesh. I could have cried then. The flies were besieging us both now and

51

I had to stop to wipe them off my face and I wished that Angus would appear and hold the wire for me while I cut it. The sun had moved so I knew that far more than an hour had passed since we parted, but at last the wire was cut away and I cried, "Up, Phantom, come on up."

He tried three times, before at last he was standing on all four legs blowing through his nostrils as though he had been galloping. The wire had left deep cuts and punctures, a perfect breeding ground for tetanus, and small pieces were still embedded in his flesh. He did not want to move. I shouted at him and hit him with the headcollar rope and then he lurched forward like an old person stiff in the joints.

"We're going home," I said. "Come on."

I decided to leave Pelican as he looked peaceful enough grazing. I walked slowly dragging Phantom and Frances after me. He'll never make the 'plane, I thought. They won't accept him. He was limping on his near fore, and his off fore seemed little better. His sides were tucked up and his mane matted with sweat and earth and blood. Then he raised his head and stopped and I saw that Angus was galloping towards us waving and shouting, "Jolly good. Where's Pelican?"

I stopped and waited for him. The blood was drying on Phantom's legs, leaving a crust on the cuts.

Angus halted the bay mare. "What's the matter?" he shouted. "What's happened to Phantom?"

The bay mare was dripping sweat on to the dry earth and I thought how hard we had used the Millers' horses and felt guilty.

"He was caught up in wire," I yelled. "His legs are ruined. He'll never make a show horse now, and he'll

52

probably get tetanus, because it must be more than ten hours since he fell into the wire."

Angus had dismounted. He looked at Phantom and sighed, "Of all the doggone luck!"

"I must have broken a mirror," I told him. "I've had nothing but bad luck for days now. Pelican is just over there. "We'll have to lead him back along the highway later. There's no other way out of the field."

It was as though someone else was speaking, someone more sensible and practical than myself.

"I'll go on ahead and telephone the vet," Angus said, remounting the bay mare. "Phantom looks awful and so do you."

I wanted to say "Thanks a million," but the words stuck in my throat. I watched Angus gallop away leaving a cloud of dust behind him and I started to hate the valley, the blistering heat, the soulless procession of cars roaring along the highway. Suddenly there seemed no point in anything any more. I started to wish that I had never set eyes on Phantom, had never caught him. Then I looked at him and saw how large his eye was, how wide his cheek. I saw his matted mane, his tail which he still carried as though on a parade ground, his neat hoofs, covered with blood and dust and I cried, "I'm going to get you home to England somehow. I swear to God I am."

Presently I could see Angus coming back, waving his arms and shouting, "The vet's coming right away. I told him about the possibility of tetanus. He says there's no time to lose. Can't you hurry?"

"I'm trying to," I replied, "but he can't walk any faster. Can't you see he's lame?"

Angus dismounted from the bay mare. "Mummy

says if he's really lame you will have to leave him behind," he told me. "There's only two more days."

"As if I didn't know." I answered and now I could see Mountain Farm, looking tiny in the distance with Mummy standing at the yard gate waiting for us. I was very hungry now and my toes were raw again, so I took my shoes off and walked the rest of the way barefoot, though Angus did his best to persuade me to ride.

The vet arrived before we did, parking his car in front of the stables. He was called Dr. Beecher, because vets in Virginia have doctor in front of their names. He was small with dark hair and he had visited us once before when I had brought Phantom home sick from the mountains. It had been winter then.

Dr. Beecher watched us limping home. "So it's that darned horse again," he cried. "He looks a heck of a lot better than he did last year."

Angus was leading Frances now. "Why don't you ride?" he asked. "You look idiotic walking without shoes."

I shook my head. I could not explain how I felt. I think I wanted to share some of Phantom's pain.

Mummy looked at my bare feet and said, "Oh, Jean . . ." Dr. Beecher bent down to look at Phantom's forelegs. He made a tut-tutting noise before he said, "Put him in the barn. I'll get my case."

The sun was moving towards the west. The air was full of midges. The stable needed mucking out. Daddy was not home yet. I wondered what he would say when he saw Phantom.

"Hold fast, little horse," said Doctor Beecher returning with a syringe, wiping a patch on Phantom's neck with a piece of cotton wool. I spoke to Phantom as the needle went into his neck and he hardly moved, only braced himself and then relaxed as the needle came out again. "Now another one; Penicillin this time," Dr. Beecher said, "and I'll dress his legs next. He's made a real picnic of them."

Angus muttered, "Some picnic." Mummy offered to fetch some water. I didn't feel like talking any more. I kept seeing a 'plane leaving without Phantom, and wondering who would be looking after him then, dressing his legs, feeding him . . . what would happen to him when I had to leave in two days time?

Mummy was talking now. Dr. Beecher was winding elastoplast round Phantom's legs. Angus had turned Frances and the bay mare out into the field near the highway.

"Will he be all right to fly in two days time?" she asked. "We've booked a flight for him from New York. We are going home."

Dr. Beecher didn't say anything for what seemed like minutes, but which can't have been more than ten seconds, then he said, "He's going to be real stiff tomorrow, and there's still a chance of tetanus. I wouldn't give him a lot of chance," he replied. "Can't it be postponed?"

Mummy started to explain and her voice seemed to go on and on for ever. Angus returned and I gave him the thumbs down sign. Phantom's legs were bandaged now, so I took off his headcollar and fetched him a bucket of water and then a feed.

Dr. Beecher got into his car. "I'll stop by tomorrow," he said. "But call me up if he gets any fresh symptoms." His tyres left marks in the dust of the drive. The frogs were croaking again and from somewhere came the lowing of a cow on and on as though she had lost her calf.

"I don't know what we are going to do. You must be starved," Mummy said. "And Daddy will be home in a minute and I don't know what he'll say."

"It wasn't my fault," I replied more from habit than anything else; because I knew whose fault it was didn't alter anything.

"I would like to murder those men who left the gate open," my brother said.

Mummy made tea. I sat with my head in my hands. "I can't leave him behind," I said.

"If he gets tetanus they'll put him down. There isn't a cure," Mummy said. "Not a permanent one."

"Why not?" I cried. *"People* aren't put down when they get it."

"Dr. Beecher says horses tend to get brainstorms afterwards and that can be very dangerous if you're riding them. He says it might be different if Phantom was a mare, because then you could raise a foal."

"I'm going to nurse him anyway," I cried. "I'm not going home till he can come too."

Mummy pushed a mug of hot tea towards me. She looked very tired. I saw that the packing cases had gone from the hall, the cookery book from the dresser. Everything left in the house besides ourselves and our clothes and a couple of cases belonged to the Millers.

"You can't stay on," Mummy said. "I won't let you. Anything could happen to you here on your own."

"Such as?" I asked.

But Mummy was looking out of the window now. "Daddy's home. He's looking at Phantom," she said.

I rushed outside. Daddy was coming towards the back door. "For goodness sake what's happened to that horse now?" he asked. He was carrying a despatch case and had taken off his tie. He took a clean white handkerchief from the breast pocket of his jacket and mopped his face.

"Why's he so lame? He doesn't know which leg to stand on," he asked.

"Come inside," replied Mummy. "There's been another disaster."

"Not another!" exclaimed Daddy. "I can't stand much more."

I followed them in. Angus looked grave. We went into the sitting room, which seemed set for disaster with all our bits and pieces missing, dust collecting, the floor dirty, waiting for a final wash before we left. We all sat down, watching the midges outside, and I wondered why everything always seemed so still when the day was hottest.

"Did you have the vet? What did he say?" Daddy asked, sipping the tea Mummy had poured for him.

"He's coming again tomorrow."

"But the horse can't walk!" exploded Daddy. "Haven't you any eyes? I tell you he can't walk. He's as sore as hell . . ."

"I know," Mummy answered.

"I shall have to put off the flight. He can't travel like that. He'll have to stay here. I'm sorry, Jean, but that's life." Daddy stood up spilling tea while I felt despair and a sick sort of rage growing inside me until I was forced to cry, "I'm not going home then. I'm not going without Phantom."

I don't know when I started to cry but when the tears came they were a relief, like the fall of rain after a hot, humid day. "I'm not going. I refuse absolutely," I cried. "I'm going to stay here and nurse him. I refuse to leave. I refuse." I don't know how many times I shouted, "I refuse." Finally Daddy said, "Go to bed, and stay there, you obstinate child," and I stumbled upstairs through blinding tears to my small bedroom which looked out on the stable at the back. I couldn't see Phantom. I supposed he was lying down. I sat on my bed and contemplated my future and there seemed no way out of anything, just endless frustration and disappointment. I could hear my parents still talking downstairs. My room smelt empty already and I saw that my few books had gone, the drawers in my chest of drawers were almost devoid of clothes, the lampshade I had chosen one sunny day in Washington had been replaced by the tasselled one which had been there when we arrived.

I thought, there must be some way out. Life can't be as awful as this. There must be a horse hospital somewhere where they could nurse Phantom and then afterwards dispatch him home. He might not load, but there must be some way of loading difficult horses. Perhaps they are drugged and loaded by crane.

I went to the bathroom and washed my face. Then I walked softly downstairs and saw that my parents were drinking sherry in the garden.

"There must be a horse hospital somewhere," I said walking towards them. "Couldn't Phantom go there and then be sent home?"

"At ten pounds a week or more," replied Daddy bitterly. "We haven't that sort of money, can't you understand? We're not rich Americans," he added, "just poor Britishers. I wouldn't be allowed the dollars to keep Phantom here week after week either, even if I had them, which I haven't."

I looked at him and I knew that he was trapped too, we were all trapped by circumstances we could not escape.

"We feel awful too," Mummy said.

It was very hot now; it was going to be hot all night. It was the sort of evening when you long for a swimming pool of your own.

I went round to the stable and looked at Phantom. He was lying down looking drowsy with his forelegs bent neatly under him. I had rarely seen him lying down in the stable before. Then I saw that Frances was missing from the paddock and I thought, oh no, not another catastrophe! I rushed to the tack room and her tack had gone too, so that I thought, she's been taken by Angus, but why on earth? And why not the bay mare? I rushed to the front of the house crying, "Have you seen Angus? Frances has gone," and then I could have bitten my tongue off for speaking at all.

"Oh no," shouted Daddy, "He hasn't gone too. This is the end, the absolute end."

"He must have gone to the Millers," Mummy answered. "I told him not to telephone. I didn't want them bothered, so rather than defy me, he's gone by horse."

"But why?" I cried. "Why did he go?" And then suddenly I knew. He had gone to seek their help. They would be home by now after their day in Washington.

"We can't let them help," said Daddy, coming to the same conclusion. We can't possibly accept any more help from them, we are too much in their debt already."

Chapter Six

We waited a long time for Angus's return, but he came at last, riding through the dusk leading Pelican like a traveller of long ago coming home.

"I hope you weren't worried," he called.

Frances was tired. Her ears flopped dully backwards and forwards as she trotted and I could see her eyes looked sullen.

Daddy was lying upstairs on his bed. Supper was over. Angus dismounted. "I've brought Pelican and the Millers will have us to stay," he said looking at Mummy. "Everything is fixed up. You can go home without us and we'll follow later with Phantom." His face looked firm set in the gathering darkness. He seemed older suddenly as he led Frances towards the stables.

"But that will mean another cancellation," Mummy said slowly. "We are spending a fortune on cancellations. Daddy's just cancelled Phantom's booking, and who will see you off? And will you be all right travelling on your own?"

"Of course!" I replied. "Don't fuss, Mummy. We are quite old now." I imagined the Millers seeing us off, New York growing smaller, and then hours later England, small and green in the midst of the Atlantic. "I shall miss you terribly," I told Mummy. "I always do, but I can't leave Phantom behind."

Angus had joined us now. "They were marvellous,"

he said. "They really are true friends. Wendy is actually looking forward to having us. The only problem is school—we've left. What are we going to do?"

"Stay away," I replied.

"We will have to discuss it with Daddy," Mummy replied. "Everything has been changed so often that I feel as though I was in the maze at Hampton Court. I don't know how we can go home without you. As for school, you're going to the new comprehensive school; it's very up to date, and I don't think a few days away from school will make much difference as to what subjects you study."

"Why didn't you tell us before? I thought we were going back to our dreary boarding schools," I asked.

"It was only decided a few days ago," Mummy replied. "Do come inside now; it's terribly late, and I've got to clean the house tomorrow."

"We'll help," Angus said. "I'm a wizard at washing floors."

"I'll polish the furniture and clean the windows," I added, wondering what the new comprehensive school would be like, whether I would quarrel with Wendy, where I would sleep.

"We'll see you off," Angus told Mummy; "then we'll catch the coach back here; it stops at the corner. I've discussed everything with Wendy." He was lit up by excitement; he couldn't stop talking; even when he was in bed he kept shouting from across the passage. "What do you think Daddy will say?" he asked, and then, "You're not to quarrel with Wendy and we've both got to help, make our beds, you know what I mean."

"I always do make my bed," I answered. "It's you who doesn't."

"Phantom's going to have the best box. They are sending the truck for him as soon as he's better."

"When he's better we are going home," I replied. "By the first available plane." I was almost asleep, but Angus's voice went on and on. Occasionally he called, "Are you listening?" and I managed a sleepy, "Yes," but I wasn't; I was seeing myself entering a classroom with plate glass windows, smiling at the other pupils, trying to be interested in English history again. Then my mind switched to the journey home. Would we both be allowed to travel on the plane with Phantom? I had never flown before—we had come by ship. The future seemed full of frightful difficulties. Downstairs the clock in the hall struck twelve and then mercifully I slept.

. . . . . .

The next morning dawned heavy with the promise of thunder. Phantom was standing up in his box, his forelegs swollen to the elbow. With shaking heart I looked for symptoms of tetanus; but he could move his head easily and his neck wasn't stiff.

"I don't think he's got it," I cried charging into the kitchen. "His legs are awful but he isn't stiff otherwise and he's eating."

Daddy was spooning marmalade onto toast in a very English manner. "So you plan to stay with the Millers now?" he asked. "You're not coming with us?"

"I can't think of anything else to do," I replied.

"I wash my hands of you then," Daddy said. "If

that darned horse matters more than coming home with us, stay here as long as you like."

I knew he was tired. I didn't know what to say and then without warning he started to laugh. "Oh, it doesn't matter," he cried. "It will give your mother and me a chance to have a few days alone together." And I started to laugh as well with a sense of relief.

Angus and I spent the morning washing the floors and helping our parents pack. They were leaving next day in the afternoon, handing the car to a dealer in Washington, taking a taxi to the Airport. I didn't want them to go now.

I had stayed with the Millers before when Angus fell off in the mountains and went to hospital. Annie did all the rough work and much else besides; and breakfast was a gracious cooked meal eaten in the dining room.

At two o'clock Dr. Beecher called again. "How is he?" he asked. "No tetanus?"

We shook our heads and took him to the stable. He knelt in the straw. "They're darned swelled, aren't they?" he asked feeling his legs. "Will he move?"

"Not much," I said.

"He'll be okay in a week I guess," Dr. Beecher told us. "Try not to worry. He'll be marked, but he'll be sound and you can take him back home to your little welfare state and hunt him."

"It's not just a welfare state," Angus answered. "London is the most important capital in the world. Virginians keep calling it little, I don't know why."

"Oh sure," replied Dr. Beecher, shutting the stable door, "it's a great country."

"He won't be here after tomorrow," I said. "We're moving him to the Millers' place."

"Okay, I'll call there the day after tomorrow then to cut off the dressings." He got into his car and drove away.

"That's another twenty dollars gone west," my brother said.

"Are you sure it's as much as that?"

"I expect so. Even an injection of Penicillin costs more than ten dollars," he replied.

"Do you think he really meant England was a great country?" I asked.

Angus shook his head. "No. They all think she's finished. Wendy says she'll be the next American state. She says they are buying it up bit by bit and one day we'll wake up and find they own it."

I started to groom Phantom. His coat shone like pale gold, his skin rippled under the body brush. I thought of Americans owning England, moving into Sparrow Cottage, sending us to live in a town. It was three o'clock already, soon our parents would be gone. I must not quarrel with Wendy whatever she said, however many times she called England "your crabby little island", or said that the men were stuffed shirts. When I was at home I grumbled about everything like everyone else, but in the States I was filled with a tremendous sense of patriotism.

Phantom walked round his box now, slowly and painfully, like an old man on sticks. I filled his water bucket and a hay net.

"We had better go inside and help some more. Mummy is getting into one of her panics," Angus said.

We ate a high tea in the kitchen. Our parents were dressed ready for their plane. "Aren't you going to change?" Mummy asked, looking at our jeans.

"We are good enough for the Greyhound coach," Angus replied.

"But not for the taxi," Mummy said.

I put on a cotton skirt, checked blouse and mocassins. Angus put on shorts and a tee shirt. Our clothes were packed ready to be dropped at the Millers' when we picked up Wendy in half an hour's time. I was feeling sick now with apprehension. Supposing Mummy and Daddy crash? I thought. Who will we live with then? It was too awful to contemplate—even Phantom was not worth such catastrophe.

Our parents were both in suits. Mummy wore a linen one with a frilly blouse underneath. She looked beautiful. Suddenly it was as though I was seeing her for the first time, as an ordinary person, instead of as my mother. We helped carry the cases to the car. Daddy locked up Mountain Farm. He walked towards the car without looking back.

Mummy said, "It was nice while it lasted. I'm glad we came, anyway."

Wendy kept us waiting. She appeared at last out of the front door in a dress with buckles at the shoulders.

It was very hot all the way to Washington. I spent the time wishing Wendy had not come. There were lots of things I wanted to say to Mummy but not in front of Wendy and I felt angry with Angus for asking her. Mummy and Daddy talked about shopping on their way home from London Airport. It made me feel homesick. I imagined them walking into homely grocers, buying English food, English greens, cauliflowers, new potatoes. Wendy and Angus made jokes. Everything was 'cute' or 'nuts' or 'fruity as a

65

c

fruit cake.' We were in Alexandria now. Time was passing quickly.

Mummy started to tell us what not to do. "Don't ride without hats," she said. "Don't ride alone. Don't take lifts from strange men. Help with the washing up. Make your beds. Be polite. . . ."

We were over the Potomac river now. We could see the Pentagon laid out like a model city. "This is where we leave the car," said Daddy a moment later.

I wasn't going to cry, not in front of Wendy. Angus was still laughing.

We left the car in exchange for a large handful of dollar bills. Daddy gave Angus and myself each a twenty dollar bill before putting the rest in his wallet. "That's to last you till you get home, so don't spend it all at once," he said hailing a cab.

"Where to?" asked the driver.

"To the airport," Daddy answered.

"Send us a cable when Mr. Miller has booked your flight home," Mummy told us as we sped through Washington. "We'll send a horsebox to meet you. I expect it will be Mr. Price."

I nodded. It seemed impossible that we would ever reach England with Phantom.

The airport was full of people carrying bags. The departure of planes was being announced over a loudspeaker.

"Ours is leaving half an hour late. There's no point in your staying," Daddy said.

"It only means prolonging the agony," Mummy agreed kissing me quickly on the cheek before turning to do the same to Angus.

Daddy found us a cab. None of us felt like speaking

now, though Wendy tried a few jokes in an effort to cheer us. "Be good," Mummy said as we climbed into the taxi.

"To the Coach Station," Daddy told the driver. "Be seeing you."

They stood waving, looking heartbreakingly familiar and for one awful moment I thought, even Phantom isn't worth this. Then Wendy slapped my shoulder. "Don't look so darned sad," she cried. "You'll be seeing them again in no time."

"If they don't crash into the Atlantic," I replied.

"You're nuts," Wendy replied. "Planes are going backwards and forwards all day long. Didn't you know? Folks wouldn't fly in them if they crashed into the sea."

We had a half-hour wait at the coach station. We sat on a bench watching people leaving for far-away places.

"I wonder if I shall ever see Miami," Angus sighed. "Or California, or San Francisco. . . ."

"Or the Rockies," I added, imagining myself riding Phantom through a mountain pass.

Wendy made friends with a boy wearing running shoes, shorts and a white tee shirt with the name of a club on it.

She said he was cute, and they exchanged addresses, sitting with their heads very close together, while I sat wondering whether Phantom had emptied his water bucket yet.

When the coach came we bagged a seat in the front. Wendy was still talking about the boy she had met, and Angus had become gloomy and rather cross.

"This coach should have left five minutes ago," he said. "Why are American coaches always late?"

And that started one of those endless arguments, England versus U.S.A., which lasted until we reached Virginia, which was full of the smell of box wood and new made hay and lit by the evening sun.

We climbed out of the coach at the top of the Millers' drive. I turned left towards Mountain Farm, while Angus and Wendy started to walk down the drive towards the Millers' house, grumbling because there was no one to meet them.

I was pleased to be walking on my own across the valley. It gave me time to contemplate the future. Phantom greeted me with a whinny. He still had food and water and, miraculously, his forelegs had started to go down. I kept my eyes averted from the house. I mucked him out and fed him, tacked up Frances and rode away across the valley and suddenly I wasn't missing my parents at all; I was filled with a great sense of happiness. This is life, I thought. I'm living. I'm five thousand miles from home and in a few days I shall be flying with Phantom and Angus, miles and miles above the sea. Suddenly all my dreams seemed possible. I imagined myself riding Phantom at Madison Square Garden, at Windsor, in Toronto and my future seemed as boundless as the universe.

Chapter Seven

The Millers were waiting dinner for me. I turned Frances into the orchard beyond the stable yard. Their dogs greeted me, running round in circles and

68

yapping. I found Annie dishing up in the kitchen.

"Do you like ice cream?" she asked. "Mrs. Miller says I make it real good, so I made it especially for you."

"I love it. Thank you very much," I answered. "Am I terribly late?"

She shook her head. "Dinner's just going in now," she answered.

We ate graciously, with candles on the table which weren't lit. Angus had washed his hands and done his hair. He sat opposite Wendy, cracking jokes, making everyone laugh. I wished that Pete was with us. Mr. Miller asked me about Phantom and I told him how he had improved already. The evening sun shone through the Georgian windows and suddenly everything seemed dated, old-fashioned, as though we had moved into some earlier age.

After dinner Wendy and I played the piano in the large drawing room which was hardly ever used. Angus talked to Mr. and Mrs. Miller in the library which had a shelf full of books about riding and leather-covered armchairs. It was all very pleasant but seemed far removed from home and Sparrow Cottage.

"They must be still flying," I said presently. "Isn't it fantastic?"

I shared Wendy's room, which had windows on both sides, with gay checked curtains and white furniture and white-wood beds with checked covers. Angus was sleeping in the spare room, which was above the drawing room and had a white carpet and a magnificent white and gold bed. It wasn't his sort of room, not a room for jeans and moccasins at all.

Wendy and I talked for hours. She told me all about a boy she had known last year. He had written her long letters. "He was the best boy-friend I ever had," she said. "I guess your brother is all right and he's real cute, but he's kinda backward, isn't he?"

I agreed. "We are all kinda backward back home," I said with a laugh. "It's something to do with the fog and being so shut in." Wendy took me seriously, while I was laughing inside all the time.

"Yeah, it must make a difference," she said. "All that rain. . . ."

I slept at last and didn't dream.

The sun was streaming into the room when I wakened and I thought straight away, they'll be home. They'll be stepping out of a car, unlocking the front door and the apple trees will be in blossom. And I wished I was there too, standing in the soft English air with the trees all pink with blossom and the banks still yellow with the last of the primroses.

Wendy was still asleep, her red-brown hair spread across her pillow.

I got up and dressed and found Annie making waffles in the kitchen.

"You want yours now? You want to get out real quick?" I nodded, wondering how she understood. I sat down at the plain wood table and she gave me a plate of waffles, crisp fried bacon and maple syrup.

"You wanta see your little horse?" she said.

Later I tacked up Frances and rode across the valley to Mountain Farm. Phantom had upset his water bucket and the house looked deserted as though it knew already that we would never be back. The hammock swung empty on the lawn. The doors were locked and bolted. "I'm taking you to the Millers' place," I told Phantom.

I led him out, and he tottered for a time and I thought, he's never going to be sound again, and my heart seemed to be beating twice as fast. Then the stiffness wore off and he looked almost sound as I rode Frances and led him across the valley. I didn't look back at Mountain Farm, because its very emptiness seemed to reproach me, as though somehow it was all my fault. Angus was waiting on the lawn in front of the house. "You might have waited. I wanted to come too. What about Pelican?" he shouted.

"I couldn't wait," I answered. "I had to see to Phantom. He had kicked over his water bucket. Where's Wendy?"

"Getting up," Angus replied.

The Millers' stables were like old-fashioned English ones with wood partitions and doors with bars. But the wood was not varnished and the bars were unpainted and the floors were beaten earth instead of Staffordshire brick. I put Phantom into one of them and he stood by the window at the back of the box trying to see out. I untacked Frances and put her back in the orchard. Beyond the orchard the last of the hay was being carted. Inside I found Wendy dressed for school.

"Of all the crabby arrangements," she said. "Why should I go while you stay home?"

Mrs. Miller drove her to school in the Pontiac with the hood down. Angus and I sat in the sun chewing grass and talking. Time hardly seemed to be passing. Peace seemed absolute; there was no point in doing anything.

"Phantom will be all right to fly in a couple of

days," I said. "Are we to make the arrangements?"

"No, Mr. Miller is going to do it," replied Angus. "You'll have to tell him."

"I wonder where Mummy is?"

"Shopping, I expect."

We took our shoes off and lay on our backs staring up into the sky.

"I shall miss this," Angus said.

"Same here. One sort of expects the sun all the time here," I answered.

"We'll be wearing jerseys again," Angus said, "and riding coats, and there won't be scorching central heating."

"But we'll be free," I answered. "We won't feel like poor relations any more." I stood up. "We'll be in our own country. It will be our turn to show people around for a change."

I walked to the stables and groomed Phantom. The boxes were mucked out straight onto a midden outside. Sometimes the midden reached nearly to the stable door, which the Millers always shut at night, so in summer unless the windows were open, the boxes were stiflingly hot. Wendy insisted that the floors were good for the horses' legs. "Much better than your crabby concrete ones," she would say.

I gave Phantom some maize still on the cob and filled his rack with hay. I fetched him water and wandered up to the house, and it still wasn't lunch time. Angus was lying in a hammock reading a book. Mrs. Miller had gone to the bank. There seemed all the time in the world.

"I wish Mr. Miller was here. I want to get everything fixed up," I said.

"Dr. Beecher has to give the O.K. What's the

matter?" asked Angus. "Why don't you read or something?"

"There's nothing to read," I replied. "All the horsy books are out of date. They are full of people with old-fashioned hunting seats and diagrams of bearing reins."

"Can't you read anything but horsy books?" asked Angus.

"Not at the moment," I replied, and then, "Supposing Phantom doesn't load, what shall I do with him? It will be worse without Mummy and Daddy. I mean Daddy can always get round people, but Mr. Miller will probably say, 'He's nutty, Jean, he'll never make good, not that darned horse, better put a bullet through his head'. . . ." As I spoke I saw Phantom's beautiful head in my mind and started to sniff.

Angus put down his book. "For goodness' sake," he replied. "Stop crapping. I've told you, they'll drug him, so what the heck?"

"You're talking American, not English at all, do you realise that?" I asked. "People will call you Yankee when you get home."

I was being irritating on purpose and suddenly I knew why; there was another storm blowing up. The air was heavy and humid. The cattle were leaving the valley for the shelter of the mountains. I wandered inside and watched Annie making rolls for lunch. She was singing softly and she kept smiling at me as she worked.

The storm broke while we were having lunch. Mr. Miller was still out.

"I guess you're a bit dull without the boys and Wendy, but she'll be back," Mrs. Miller said.

Angus was in one of his chatty moods. He talked

all through lunch, making Mrs. Miller laugh, and now the rain was falling in drops as big as hailstones, drenching the valley in seconds.

Wendy returned later cross from school. "Doggone it, it isn't fair," she shouted. "Why should you stay home, while I work myself nutty in that crabby school."

Mr. Miller was home by this time and we all wandered round to the stables together to look at Phantom.

"A cable came through from your parents a few minutes ago," Mr. Miller told us. "It said, *Home safe, love, Mummy and Daddy.*"

"Super," said Angus.

I imagined them sending it, sitting in our tiny hall and telephoning while as likely as not rain fell through the trees outside.

Mr. Miller wanted to cut away Phantom's bandages, but we persuaded him to leave it until tomorrow when Dr. Beecher would come.

"He looks okay, Jean," he said. "I'll book you a plane next week. What's today?"

"Thursday," I answered, after a pause for reflection, for the days had become muddled and in some strange way pointless now.

"Monday then," said Mr. Miller slamming the box door shut. "He'll be fit enough then and I'll sure be glad to see the back of him, yes siree, the trouble that horse has caused."

"If he loads," Wendy replied.

"He'll load. They'll see to that, else it will be the humane killer," replied Mr. Miller. "We sure don't want him roaming the mountains again."

There was a red sun going down in a glorious pool

74

of colour beyond Mountain Farm. The sky was red and gold and blue, the grass sparkling with raindrops.

"You won't see anything like this in England," Wendy told me.

I nodded agreement. Annie was waiting for us with dinner on the table. There were gleaming glasses and starched napkins in silver rings. The table was polished until you could see your face in it. The mahogany chairs had seats covered with striped brocade.

The Millers are going to find Sparrow Cottage very small after this, I thought. Phil will hit his head on the beams and the chair in the hall will break under Mr. Miller's weight. But it will be lovely having them all the same. I will be able to show Wendy my books and Mermaid's rosettes, and, if they come in September, the apples will be ripe. I saw myself taking them to the village shop; old Mrs. Pratt peering at them through her spectacles, saying, "You're not from these parts," in her old cracked voice.

The next day Angus and I rode up to the mountains. We crossed the gas line and stood at Signal Post where George Washington was supposed to have stood, and we stared into the distance seeing the Potomac river running like a thread through the landscape.

"Do you remember seeing all this for the first time?" Angus asked. "I've grown kinda fond of it, haven't you?"

"Yes," I said, "I want to remember every bit of it for ever, even the smell, but I don't suppose I will. But one day I shall come back."

"Same here," said Angus picking up his reins again.

We rode down to find Dr. Beecher waiting for us in the yard.

"I've seen the little horse," he told us as we dismounted. "He's sure made a wonderful recovery. I should give him another day or two before you take him back home. I've given him another shot of Penicillin, he'll be okay now. Put him out in the orchard this evening."

"Thank you very much. Can he go without his bandages?" I asked.

"Sure. Just one other problem. What about the account?"

"The account?" I said stupidly.

"Sure, here it is. I thought you'd like it before you go back home."

I opened the envelope Dr. Beecher gave me. Inside I read *Two visits. Four injections, 40 dollars*, only it wasn't written quite like that.

"Yes," I said, "yes' of course," while my mind thought, forty dollars—fifteen or more pounds, and reeled at the thought.

Angus looked over my shoulder and nudged me. "We've got forty dollars inside," he said. "Hang on."

We paid Dr. Beecher and watched him drive away. "Wow, what a price!" I said. "We haven't a penny for the journey now."

"Exactly; that darned horse, he'll be the ruin of us," Angus was laughing. "Who cares anyway?" he asked. "We'll manage."

I wished I was more like him then, instead of always seeing ahead, working things out before I reached them, perpetually fearing the worst. Mummy says you're born one way or the other, but I think it's more an attitude of mind and if you can train anything you ought to be able to train your own mind.

I couldn't hold Phantom when I led him into the

I opened the envelope Dr. Beecher gave me

yard in the evening. He stood on his hind legs, snatching the headcollar rope from my hands and careered away across the yard.

"Fool!" shouted Angus. "Idiot. Why didn't you hold on?"

"I couldn't," I shouted. "I tried."

Phantom tore round the yard in a mad frolic. Then he cleared the gate into the orchard in one quick leap and settled down to eat. I sighed with relief.

"If only we can keep him safe till Monday," I said.

"And in the plane. You know it will be pressurised, either a DC 10 or a Boeing. If he puts a hoof through the fusilage we will all die," Angus said.

The next day we rode again and Mr. Miller told us that the flight was booked and Phantom would be flying with some brood mares on Monday evening. "It's a chartered flight," he said. "One of the mares can't go, so he'll be in a box by himself. I told them he was a heck of a horse. I sure hope he behaves."

I could think of nothing but the flight now. It seemed to dominate everything. I imagined a thousand things going wrong.

The Millers were wonderful. They took us swimming and to Charlottesville and to an outdoor performance of The Barber of Seville. Pete and Phil came home on Sunday and we had a farewell dinner with wine, and an enormous rib roast, and fresh corn bread and gallons of ice cream, and salads of pineapple, mayonnaise, lettuce and cottage cheese. It was all very Virginian and I was suddenly overcome by the sadness of leaving. Virginia had never seemed so beautiful before, the Millers never nicer.

We were still up when the moon rose and the dark sky was filled with millions of stars like jewels on dark velvet.

"We'll be over in July," Pete told me. "It will sure be good to see you again."

I didn't want the day to end. I kept thinking, I may never come again, this could be my last evening in Virginia.

Wendy wanted to know what she should wear in England. "Skirts are real short, aren't they?" she asked. "And the boys wear frilly shirts."

Phantom tore round the yard

At last we retired to bed, but I couldn't sleep. It seemed impossible that this time tomorrow we would be flying to England with Phantom, it seemed too impossible to come true.

Pete and Phil had gone back to their Military Academy. The air was full of sounds unheard in England. I opened one of the windows and leaned out remembering again the first time I had seen Phantom galloping wild and alone across the moonlit valley; somehow even then I had been certain that one day he would be mine.

Chapter Eight

Monday morning dawned fine.

"I'm coming with you. I'm not going to school, no siree," cried Wendy leaping out of bed. "I want to see Phantom load. Daddy's coming too."

I was dressing slowly, saying goodbye to everything, already feeling the heat of the sun through the windows. Angus was still asleep. Phantom had spent the night in the orchard and he was still there, scarred but sound, waiting by the gate. Mrs. Miller helped us pack, putting everything in plastic bags with tissue paper between the folds. Tomorrow I shall be in England, I thought, and it still didn't seem possible.

"Charlie's sent your parents a cable," Mrs. Miller told us. "And Charlie and Wendy are travelling with you to New York. The horse box is coming after lunch."

There was a funny feeling in my stomach now, as though it was full of fluttering butterflies.

"We can't possibly repay you for everything; you've been super," said Angus in a grown-up voice.

"We don't want repaying, it's been a pleasure," replied Mrs. Miller.

Annie was making cookies for us to eat on the journey. I felt then that the Millers were the best friends we had ever had, our only real friends.

I caught Phantom and groomed him. Then Angus and I went round the other horses saying goodbye. I stood for ages with my arms round Frances's neck remembering the days and hours we had shared together. Then I said goodbye to Easter and Seashore and Pete's dun mare, and Pelican and Phil's new black hunter. Then I returned to Frances and said goodbye all over again. And all the while, time was passing relentlessly and the worst part of the journey still lay ahead, waiting like some fearful ordeal to be overcome.

Lunch was hot dogs—onion and frankfurters inside toasted rolls—followed by more ice cream. I wanted to ask Mr. Miller for some money, but Angus said that we could beg no more and where was my pride? The day was at its hottest now. Phantom was sweating in the stable. Wendy found some slightly moth-eaten bandages in the saddle room and gave them to me. I put them on Phantom's forelegs. I was wearing jodhpurs and was far too hot. I was trying to look like a responsible person. Angus was dressed in grey trousers and a shirt and tie. Wendy wore jeans, moccasins and a tee shirt.

"It'll be kinda funny without you around," she said with a break in her voice.

"It will be funnier still to see you on our crabby

little island," Angus replied and we all laughed because he made England sound like our own private property.

But now the horsebox was coming across the cattle grid to the yard. Annie was standing on the steps outside the laundry room waving goodbye.

"We should have got her some chocolates," muttered Angus.

"We'll send her something super from England, a dress or something," I replied, and all the time I felt as though my heart was breaking, because I was leaving the dusty valley with the rock-hard ground and the Blue Ridge Mountains in the distance.

The driver of the horsebox was letting down the ramp. He was a big, sweaty man in a grubby white tee shirt which clung to his back in the heat, and light-coloured trousers.

"I'll take him," he said looking at me.

I had led Phantom out by this time and he stood all flaxen and gold in the sunshine, bursting with health.

"He doesn't like strangers, let the kid lead him up," said Mr. Miller, who had appeared dressed in riding clothes with a cloth cap on his head.

But Phantom would not budge. His head seemed to go higher and higher as though he was trying to look behind him and say goodbye to his beloved mountains. Angus fetched a scoop of oats. Annie appeared with carrots. Mrs. Miller brought sugar. The driver took him, jerking at his head and shouting, "Get up there. Someone get a rope," he said presently. "Gee, he's strong."

They fetched a rope and put it round his buttocks and pulled, while I coaxed him with the scoop in front; but he threw himself backwards after a minute's contemplation and everyone fled.

"We'll never make it," said Mr. Miller looking at his watch. "What did I tell you, Jean? He's no darned good. Someone should put a bullet in him."

I could feel the tears pricking behind my eyes now. I couldn't imagine Angus and myself returning without him; it was awful beyond words.

Then I remembered something I had seen someone else doing at a show and I cried, "Let me ride him up. He trusts me." Another minute and I was vaulting on his back while the driver was saying, "He'll kill her on the roof if he rears." And Angus was saying, "Be careful, Jean. Jump off if he goes up on his hind legs."

His coat was dark with sweat. I said, "Walk on," in the same voice as I used when I had lunged him months ago. I felt the tenseness going out of his body and I went on talking, but I can't remember what I said. I forgot the others completely; I could have been alone on a desert island—anywhere. I just continued talking and I sensed the others standing watching, no doubt thinking I was as nutty as a fruit cake. And then slowly he moved and I went on talking and now we were on the ramp and he was still walking forward, relaxed and confident, the fear drained out of him. I dismounted inside the box and someone put the ramp up. I tied up Phantom and shouted, "I'll stay here," and there were cries of "Goodbye and good luck."

It was a five-horse horsebox and most of the partitions were still up, so there was not a lot of room. I heard the cab door shut and the engine start and Angus looked at me through a window in the cab and said, "Are you all right?"

I was fighting back tears now; someone was still calling "Goodbye", and I should have been happy because the first part of the journey had begun and I was going home.

"Sure," I answered.

The drive was bumpy and I knew when we reached the highway because the box ran smoother. There were slats on the sides which I could peer through and I said goodbye to the drugstore where you could buy newspapers, writing paper, cosmetics, things you buy in a chemist and a host of other things, and have cokes there too, and hot dogs, sitting at the tables in the centre of the store.

I said goodbye to the gasoline station where we bought our gas (petrol in England) and I heard the others talking on and on in a steady drone in the cab in front.

The drive to New York seemed to last for ever. Somewhere we all got out, except for Phantom, and stretched our legs in a side road, where small houses hid behind tall trees. Phantom kept whinnying as though he feared he would be forgotten. The driver mopped his brow.

"It'll be real hot in New York," he said.

We drove on and presently there was a feeling of evening outside and through the slats I could see people going home from work—dozens of men wearing sun-glasses, women carrying shopping bags, girls in cotton dresses. Children were standing at the roadside and there was more and more traffic and larger and larger highways.

Angus passed some of Annie's cookies through the window between the cab and me. "Are you all right? Would you like to change places with me?" he asked.

I shook my head.

"It won't be long now, Jean," Mr. Miller told me.

"About another two hours," the driver said.

The traffic was building up now. There was driver after driver in white nylon shirt, his coat hanging up, listening to his car radio. Once I heard a train, another time a mother calling to her child. And now there were more houses and the fields were disappearing; then without warning, the suburban homes ceased and there were blocks and blocks of flats and skyscrapers and enormous petrol stations. It's New York, I thought, we're nearly there.

Phantom was resting a hind leg. He looked peaceful enough. There was the smell of a town outside—petrol fumes, dust, hot pavements, rotting vegetables in dustbins, sweaty humans.

We kept stopping at traffic lights and every time Phantom seemed to raise his head a little higher and grow more restless as though he too could smell the town outside. He looked very beautiful with his nostrils blown out and a wild look in his eyes.

Some of the shops were lit up already though it wasn't yet dark. Then, at last, the horsebox started to slow down and I could see grass again through the trees and low buildings, and men in uniform.

"We've arrived," shouted Angus through the opening. "And there are some super planes. Honestly Jean, gee they are marvellous."

I wasn't interested in the planes, only in one plane —Phantom's. I felt as though I had reached a turning point in my life, what Mummy would call my 'Waterloo'.

We parked by some horseboxes. My legs were stiff when I stepped out into the summer dusk.

Mr. Miller took us across the airport to a buffet room and I remember I kept saying, "What about Phantom? I don't want him scared."

"We've got an hour and a half before loading time. There's all sorts of formalities to be gone through yet. I'll see to them while you have something to eat," he replied.

Wendy brushed straw off my back. Angus was still raving over the planes, looking like grey monsters parked uneasily on the runways in the gathering dusk.

I ate three hamburgers without tasting them. Wendy and Angus talked. I don't know what they said. Then Wendy fell for a boy with dark hair and a lightweight summer suit. He had a smooth, sun-tanned face and looked like an advertisement for shaving cream. She whispered to me, "He's sure cute, isn't he?" in a perfectly audible voice and the boy turned and smiled at us in a perfect ad' for tooth paste and I felt slightly sick. Quite soon after that he and Wendy were talking and Angus made a face at me and muttered, "Oh, to be in England." And then at last Mr. Miller came back.

"The horse doctor is looking at him now," he said. "They're going to be loaded on pallets. There's a crowd of brood mares going too. It's so darned humid outside it isn't true."

The driver had unloaded Phantom. He stood like a wild horse staring round the airport. His beauty made me catch my breath.

"Gee, some horse!" exclaimed Wendy.

"He's passed his tests," the driver said. "Sure you can hold him? He's real strong."

"Sure." I took the rope and we all walked together to where three brood mares were waiting patiently to be loaded, as peacefully as people waiting for a bus. Phantom neighed when he saw them and we were told to keep him away.

"Those mares are worth three hundred thousand dollars," said a man unmistakably English.

The boxes were waiting on the ground and the mares walked into them without a murmur. A man asked Mr. Miller for Phantom's certificates and Mr. Miller passed him a handful of documents. It was really dusk now and suddenly everything felt like a vast conspiracy in the gathering darkness. Then Phantom started to jump about and neigh and the mares answered from their boxes and I felt panic growing inside me until I wanted to shout, "Please hurry, every passing minute is going to make loading more difficult."

But the official was still talking to Mr. Miller and presently the driver went to the horsebox and returned with Phantom's bridle. We had difficulty putting it on, because Phantom was whirling round and round by this time and his neck was streaked with sweat. "I'll ride him in," I said before anyone could argue.

Angus legged me up and I could feel Phantom relaxing as I walked him round and round, staring at the lights of New York beyond the airport. A plane came in to land with a roar and he trembled all over and the reins were salt wet with his sweat. But he only stared at the plane and then relaxed as I rode him towards the box. There was a sudden silence as he walked into it; then behind me Angus shouted, "Hurray, well done, Jean," and the Englishman said, "I've never seen that done before."

I dismounted and found I was trembling all over from nervous exhaustion. I took off his bridle leaving his headcollar underneath.

I was allowed out of the box while the dolly took it to the aircraft standing ready on the runway; the dolly was rolled onto a lift and slowly Phantom was raised to the height of the aircraft and the box pushed inside on rollers fixed to the floor of the plane. It was then clipped into position inside. We all sighed with relief when that was done and Wendy said, "I owe you ten dollars or was it twenty?"

And I said, "Forget it." And none of us knew how to say goodbye. Then Angus held out his hand and said, "It was good of you to come, sir. I don't know how to thank you."

And Mr. Miller took it and squeezed it until Angus's face grew red with agony. "You're welcome, Angus. Proud to have known you," he said.

Then I held out my hand and received the same treatment and suddenly, Wendy's face was covered with tears and she walked away across the airport without saying goodbye.

I ran after her. I seized her arm and said, "I'm going to thank you for everything whether you like it or not. You've saved our lives countless times in countless ways, and it's impossible to thank you enough." It sounded silly, like a bad speech on Sports Day and it didn't stop Wendy crying.

"You could have stayed a little longer," she muttered. "A few more days wouldn't have killed you."

I didn't know what to say. I thought I could hear the plane's engine starting up behind me and Angus was calling, "Come on, Jean."

"See you in July and thanks a million, million times for everything," I shouted.

I had never flown before. I was filled with a wild excitement as I approached the plane. I thought of seeing England again, of leading Phantom into the yard at home and I was filled with a sense of achievement. Mr. Miller had handed Angus a mass of documents in a case. "You'll have to handle these," he said. "Jean can only think of that darned horse. Happy landing."

We watched him disappearing. "He's not walking out of our lives, none of them are," said Angus with a choke in his voice.

Chapter Nine

It was a long time before the plane took off. We had looked at the brood mares by then. They were thoroughbreds and one had a foal at foot. Phantom was screened off from them. Two seats had been provided for Angus and me. There was a haynet for Phantom and a polythene container full of water, and two containers of food for us.

When the plane took off at last I held him by his headcollar. We seemed to be going faster and faster and then miraculously we were airborne. I kept saying, "Whoa, steady there," and I sensed that other people were saying the same to the mares. It was a perfect takeoff. Angus was wildly excited.

"New York looks wonderful," he cried. "I swear I can see Times Square and there's Manhattan and Wall Street. . . . There are masses of lights. There's clouds," he said, "but not a lot, and stars, billions of stars."

We were really in the air now. Phantom started to munch his hay. I relaxed. I let my body go limp for the first time in hours. I was too tired to feel any great sense of triumph.

"It's so smooth," Angus said. "We must be above the sea now." He kept disappearing and coming back with more information. I was fighting off sleep.

"There's a racehorse trainer on board," Angus told me. "All the grooms are English. The mares are travelling marvellously. It's practically dark and the clouds look like some fantastic sea below us." He opened one of the food containers and handed me a sandwich. "You don't seem very excited," he said.

"It's smoother than anything I've ever been on before," I answered. "And I can't see much from here, can I?" All my strength seemed to have gone. I only wanted to sit by Phantom's head and wait for England.

"There's nothing to see at present," said Angus disappearing and returning, "but one of the grooms says that sometimes you see three sunrises."

"We're much too late for one," I said.

"You mean the New York one?" asked Angus.

I had finished my sandwich. Phantom was still eating.

"Wendy and Mr. Miller will be just arriving home in the horsebox. Gee, they were swell, weren't they?" Angus said.

The temperature was regulated to suit the horses. I shivered more from fatigue than anything else.

"You go to sleep. I'll watch him. I'm not tired at all," Angus said, his eyes bright with excitement.

I shut my eyes and almost at once I was dreaming I was in Virginia again chasing Wendy, who kept shouting, "You hate me. I know you do. You always have," and then suddenly it was England. The fields were full of hay bales which Wendy jumped and Mummy was standing by a gate and clapping.

I don't know how long I slept. I dimly heard Angus talking about a sunset and Phantom pawing the floor, and English voices talking without pause as though telling their life histories, and then there was a noise like thunder and the plane seemed to tip and suddenly I was awake, sitting up, instantly aware of where I was.

Phantom was racing round his box and Angus was trying to put his bridle on. But the plane wasn't flying straight any more and Phantom was standing on his hind legs and neighing. I heard someone shout, "For God's sake quieten that horse," before I snatched the bridle from Angus and threw the reins over Phantom's head. Angus was holding onto his headcollar rope, but it didn't make much difference to Phantom, who seemed to have gone mad. I tried to hold his ear and failed and for an awful minute or more I was whirling round the box with him, my legs entangled in the reins. Then a voice said, "Let me help," and I saw the racehorse owner for the first time, looking sombre in a coat and hat like someone from a different world. "We're eight miles up," he continued. "He'll finish us all off in a minute if he doesn't stop. One foot through the fuselage and we're done for."

I had forgotten what English voices sounded like. But his voice did nothing to calm Phantom, who threw himself against the side of the box and pawed the air, and suddenly I felt as terrified as he was—one hoof through the fuselage I thought and we are all finished. And I saw us going down into the sea, the

91

wreck floating, while we had been sucked out into space. Mummy and Daddy hearing the news on television—the headlines in the papers. All this went through my mind in a flash but by then a man in uniform had appeared. "Put this on," he said, handing us oxygen masks. "And make it slippy. The captain's going to lower the temperature. It's the only thing he can do."

I couldn't get my mask on; my hands were shaking too much. But Angus knew how it went and pushed it over my head and clipped the ends together. The racehorse trainer had put his on and I saw that he was filling a hyperdermic syringe. "I'll just give him a shot of Promazine to quieten him down," he said.

Phantom was standing still now looking rather drunk. His eyes looked glazed and his ears seemed to have no life in them. I put his bridle on. The 'plane was flying normally again.

"It was just a freak storm," the trainer said slipping the syringe into Phantom's velvet skin. "Keep the bridle on for the rest of the flight. It's only another couple of hours," he said, "and stay with him." He was a big man, but he moved quietly and calmly round Phantom and one could tell he had spent most of his life with horses. He left us in the box and I heard him call, "Everything under control, Captain."

I looked at Angus and thought he looked like a character in space. My hands had stopped shaking but I felt sick. Presently a groom appeared and told us to take our masks off. He was a small wiry man. "I've never known that happen before," he said. "Is he unbroken?"

"No, just difficult," Angus replied.

I did not feel like talking. Phantom looked half

asleep. He moved unsteadily and his eyes were still peculiar. Angus had disappeared with the masks and presently he came back, saying, "I've just seen a sunrise. It's too late for England's. I don't know whose it is, but we're nearly home." And suddenly the night seemed to have lasted for ever. My teeth had started to chatter and I thought, supposing Phantom goes mad again when we touch down. But looking at him, I knew it wasn't possible, for he was too tired and dopey with the sweat drying on his sides and a far-away look in his eyes.

"We're nearly there," said the race-horse trainer. "I thought I would just let you know. You're a bit young to travel with a horse alone. You're still in your teens, aren't you? I suppose they realised I was aboard so we would be all right. He's a nice little horse though, a real American I should say."

I started to tell him Phantom's life history, but there was not enough time.

"I must go now," he said. "We'll be landing soon. The best of luck with him."

"Thank you for saving us," I replied.

"You're welcome," he answered.

I left the hold for a moment and looked out and saw England below like patchwork, the fields and houses growing larger each moment. I started to feel sick again, with excitement this time as though I had been away for years. Then I returned to Phantom and ate what was left of the food in the containers.

I knew we were losing height now but Phantom seemed hardly to notice. He stood like someone dreaming and he only moved a little as the 'plane started to reduce speed, going lower and lower until we were on the runway, still going but no longer in the air. Then almost without warning, we had stopped.

"They are going to unload your little horse last," the trainer said. "I'll keep an eye on him. You go and have a cup of coffee. He won't be out for half an hour at least."

I said, "Thank you."

Outside the grass looked very green and the sky grey, a greyer sky than we had seen for months. The Englishmen we saw looked lean and hard and sunburnt compared with Americans and the parked cars looked tiny and rather old and rusty. Everything seemed small, as though we had moved to somewhere which was made on a smaller scale.

"The air smells different," said Angus sniffing. "And we haven't any money, have we? Not even to telephone. Oh cursed fate. And I would love bacon and eggs, wouldn't you?"

It was noon. It seemed impossible but somehow we had bypassed morning altogether. And then Angus cried, "Look, look over there. Beyond the barrier. There's Mummy and Daddy, look!" And suddenly we were both running, as though our lives depended on it.

"It was a terrible journey," I shouted to Mummy. "Phantom nearly took us to the bottom of the sea."

"You can't come out yet. What about Customs?" Daddy asked.

Our baggage was being taken out of the 'plane and with it Angus's case of documents. We tore back to the runway. Some of the brood mares had been unloaded and were standing peacefully in the morning light like seasoned travellers waiting to be collected. Our luggage had been removed already, so we rushed back to Mummy and Daddy again and I thought how marvellous it was to be with them again and how we needn't worry any more. Daddy disappeared and came back with everything fixed up.

"You are coming with us," he said. "I am told you were marvellous on the 'plane, as cool as cucumbers. But I think you've suffered enough for one night. Mr. Price will load Phantom, there's plenty of people around to help and anyway he's still very docile after his tranquilliser."

Daddy had bought a car. It looked very small and I couldn't imagine the Millers sitting in it. The motorway was full of traffic and it was much smaller than I remembered.

Later I found I had forgotten how high the hedges were, how small the cottages, how green the grass. I felt as though I was seeing England properly for the first time. Angus fell asleep with his mouth open. Henley was full of traffic.

"It all looks so frightfully old," I said.

The trees were magnificent, large and thick with leaves and somehow terribly English. And all the time I still couldn't believe that we were really home, that somehow we had made it and that the night was over.

"The Millers are coming in July," I said. "They were super. Mr. Miller and Wendy saw us off. They arranged everything. I don't know how we will ever repay them."

"There's no one nicer than a nice American," Daddy said, "and Charlie always was a decent chap."

And now I knew every turn of the road; there was the corner where I had fallen off Mermaid for the first time, the rectory where I had been to the annual

Christmas party, the farm where we bought our hay and then the twisty stretch of road with high hedges and elms on each side which led home. I couldn't sit still any longer. I wanted to walk the final bit, but Daddy wouldn't stop the car. My heart started to pound against my ribs. Nothing was changed. The fields were as green as when we had left. There were birds singing in the elms, cow's parsley on the grass verges and low-branched apple trees in orchards. Then Daddy turned into the familiar drive and I saw that Mermaid and Moonlight were home, grazing in the orchard.

"We thought Phantom might like a little company so we begged them back," Mummy said.

"We don't want any more night chases," Daddy added.

The tulips were out and the rose climbing round the porch. It was all fantastically beautiful in a completely different way from the valley we had left. I wondered what the Millers would think of it when they came. Angus was awake now, climbing out of the car.

"What's the time?" he cried. "Can we ride before lunch?"

We ran together to the orchard and looked at Mermaid and Moonlight. "They're tiny," Angus said. "Much too small for us. I must have grown a mile since we were last here."

He suddenly looked tired and disheartened. "I can't ride Moonlight any more. It would be cruelty to animals," he said.

I felt sick again suddenly. I felt I had everything and it wasn't fair. "Can't we share Phantom? It was only luck that I found him. It might easily have been you," I answered.

Angus shook his head. He had his arms round Moonlight's neck. "He's yours. He always has been. I think he likes you. It's just one of those things. He and I would never get on. We are both too wild," he said.

"Perhaps Daddy will buy you a new horse," I suggested.

"Not likely. It cost a fortune bringing Phantom over, and he's just bought a car. Oh, it doesn't matter," he finished, turning towards the house. But I knew it did matter by the way he walked and suddenly everything was spoilt.

Chapter Ten

The next few days were hectic. Phantom settled down. Angus and I attended the new comprehensive school, catching the 'bus each morning at the cross-roads. I rode guiltily while Angus thought about his O levels and tried not to mind. I schooled Phantom in the small paddock behind the house and Angus made a mock ring for me out of pieces of rope and string and we put peculiar things inside, old coats on sticks, an ancient pram with a heap of rags inside, a pile of stones. And Angus dressed up and pretended to be a judge. He rang an ancient cow bell from Zermatt, and shouted, "Will entries for Class Eight, Novice Jumping for Lunatics and the Infirm, please come into the ring."

D

Phantom hesitated for a moment and then walked in, only stopping to peer at the pram.

"Ride him round," shouted Angus, "and then give him a reward." Phantom cantered round the ring like a dressage horse, or so I told myself. Then I jumped off and gave him three lumps of sugar and a whole crust of bread. I tied him up and made a few jumps— poles perched on dented oil drums, a wall out of the old scullery door, a frightful cross-bars out of bean poles which were far too fragile for a decent jump. Angus found a mackintosh and put it on the poles, then he brought out two chairs and tied some string between them and attached Mummy's tea towels to it with clothes pegs.

"I'm not very happy about jumping the chairs. I know they are only the kitchen ones, but all the same . . ." I said.

"You need only jump it once," Angus replied. "He never hits anything anyway."

He started telling me how to jump the course, while I untied Phantom and mounted. The sky was full of fluffy clouds and there was a breeze which fanned my face.

Phantom cleared the pole in the air easily. He hesitated for a moment at the scullery door and then we were over that too. He looked at the mackintosh and jumped very big and then we cantered on towards the chairs. I could feel him eyeing the tea towels. They were very gay, one had an elephant on it, another flowers, the third a pepperpot and carving knife and fork. He tried to run out, but I managed to straighten him and even now I don't know exactly what went wrong. Angus said afterwards that he turned as he jumped. I was nervous and I've always felt he knew it. Anyway, one of his hoofs caught in a chair and there was the sound of cracking wood and Angus started to shout, "Stop him, you fool. Get off."

I threw myself on to the ground but it was too late, for the chair was already a broken heap of wood on the grass.

"I told you we shouldn't use them," I cried. "I knew something awful would happen."

"You didn't ride him properly," shouted Angus, picking up the tea towels which were covered with hoof marks.

"We should have touched wood," I replied. "Whatever will Mummy say?"

I turned Phantom into the orchard and rushed indoors with the tea towels. I started to wash them at the sink and Mummy appeared.

"Whatever are you doing that for?" she asked. "They were clean ten minutes ago, and where are the kitchen chairs? I've been looking everywhere for them. I've just had a cable from the Millers; they are coming at the end of next week."

"Next week?" I shouted.

"And I shall need the chairs then, because there aren't enough for us all in the dining room."

"We've broken one of them. We were using them for jumps," Angus explained. "I'll buy you a new one out of my Post Office account. I've got four pounds in it."

"They were six guineas each from Heals," Mummy cried, running towards the paddock.

She came back slowly with the pieces of wood in one hand, the good chair in the other. I felt horribly guilty. Angus kept saying, "I'll buy you another. I'll go into Oxford or Reading on the 'bus. I'm old enough. I'll get you something super from an antique shop."

"It's not as though you're only nine or ten," Mummy said. "You are quite old. Why don't you take Phantom to the riding school? I'm sure Miss Mackintosh will let you jump her jumps."

I had learned to ride at the riding school. Miss Mackintosh was small and weatherbeaten. She had worn her hair the same way for twenty years and she was quite old now and it didn't suit her any more. But she was kind, one of the kindest people I had ever met.

"What a super idea. I'll go after lunch," I cried.

"And there's a show the week after next. You can take the Millers," she continued. "I've rung up for a schedule."

"Oh, you're wonderful," I cried. "The most wonderful mother in the world! I shall take Phantom. I shall make him go in the ring and win Mr. Miller's bet." I was dancing about with excitement now. I rushed outside with the tea towels and hung them on the line. Phantom was standing under the elms with Moonlight and Mermaid. I caught him and groomed him for forty minutes, and oiled his hoofs. It was lunch time after that and Angus and I washed up afterwards because Mummy was tired and we still felt guilty about the chairs. Then I tacked up Phantom and rode down the road towards the riding school, wondering how many dollars made a pound and whether the pound had gone up or down recently.

Miss Mackintosh was tacking up horses for the afternoon ride. She squinted up at me before she cried, "But it's Jean. You are back, and what are you riding? He's lovely."

She stood back as horsy people do when they want to look at a horse properly, and she said, "He carries himself beautifully, and he's got a wonderful shoulder. Where did you find him?"

"I brought him back with me," I said and started to tell his story.

"I can't hear it all now," she said after a minute. "I've got a class in ten minutes; but knowing you, you want to jump."

"Please. Are you sure? I mean, it seems an awful cheek," I began.

"This way," said Miss Mackintosh walking towards the five-barred gate which led to the jumping field.

"I'll put them at three foot to start with. Has he jumped that high? Or would you rather start with the cavaletti?"

"Three foot will be fine." I rode Phantom in a circle. He had never jumped proper painted show jumps before, for the ones in Virginia were plain, permanent solid fences to test hunters across country.

"Ready?" I tightened Phantom's girths and called back, "Yes."

The jumps were arranged in a figure of eight. The first one was a Sussex gate. Phantom took it in his stride; the wall came next and he cleared that too. I turned right for the red and white cross bars and he increased his speed and suddenly we were tearing round the course, one jump following another, his tail streaming behind him like a pennant and Miss Mackintosh jumping about in the middle, shouting, "Not so fast. They're nothing to him. I'll put them up a foot."

One jump followed another

"But that will make them four foot," I said drawing rein.

"So what?" she said. "If you want to jump him in novice classes he'll have to clear four foot. You had better register him with the B.S.J.A.; you've got a winner there." Her face was lit up with excitement. And I was filled with gratitude.

"There's a show the week after next. You can come with me. I'm only taking two in the box," she said.

I trusted her completely. Anything and everything seemed possible as I rode round the course again. Phantom didn't let me down. I sat on top and he took me round, jumping every fence perfectly, turning the corners like a polo pony.

"He's worth four figures without a doubt," said Miss Mackintosh, when I had dismounted and she was stuffing Phantom with oats from her pockets. "You are a very lucky girl. Ring up the show secretary tonight and see if they are taking any more entries, then ring me and let me know. There's a schedule pinned to the wall in the saddle room."

The yard was full of waiting pupils when I reached it. I put Phantom in a box and helped adjust their stirrups. Miss Mackintosh's words still rang in my ears. "He's worth four figures without a doubt."

I went round the stables with a skip and filled up the water buckets, remembering how I had haunted the stables once, and feeling immensely grateful for what Miss Mackintosh had taught me in the past.

Then after finding a piece of paper in the saddle room and writing down the show secretary's telephone number, I rode home along the grass verges. Cars slowed down for Phantom and an enormous lorry stopped completely and then eased itself past us at five miles an hour, while Phantom stood like a statue eyeing it. I'm winning that battle too. He's getting used to traffic I thought, cantering along the verge, jumping ditches and singing, imagining the Millers arriving and loving everything.

The next day was spent turning out the cottage in preparation for the arrival of the Millers. Mummy had bought a gallon of white emulsion paint and three brushes. We spread paper on everything and Angus and I painted the ceilings. When we had finished we had paint in our hair and on our faces. Mummy was painting the doors in the kitchen with a blue gloss paint. "There won't be much for lunch," she said. "Open a tin of luncheon meat and there's some lettuces in the garden. We'll have a proper dinner tonight when Daddy's home."

"I can't think why we have to bother so much about the Millers," Angus said. "They always call England a crabby little island, so they won't expect much, will they? And it's spoiling the whole of half term."

I wandered into the garden and found the lettuces our tenants had obligingly planted some time back in the spring. Next week we would start exams, and we weren't prepared for them. The exams would decide what O levels we took. If I fail them all I shall take up riding, I thought. I'll school horses and sell them. I'll tour the shows and sleep in the other half of a trailer on a camp bed. I shall never pass the history exam, nor the geography for that matter.

On my way back I brushed against the door Mummy had been painting and now my shirt had blue all down one side. Then Angus tripped over the emulsion paint and we spent nearly an hour mopping it up with newspaper, and now we all had nerves about the Millers' impending visit.

"We'll never be able to amuse them," Angus said. "We haven't any mountains round the corner, nor half a dozen horses to spare, and you can't ask Phil and Pete to play Murders."

"I don't see why not," answered Mummy. "Anyway there's the show. They'll enjoy that."

"Will they?" replied Angus. "I don't think they will. They'll think English horses are tiny."

"And I shall fall off or run away and then I shall have to pay Mr. Miller five hundred dollars and I haven't got that much money in the world," I cried and suddenly everything seemed against me again, the exams, Phantom, the painting and clearing up. "I don't believe we'll ever be ready for them. Where are they going to sleep?" I asked.

"Charlie and Ann can have our room," Mummy said. "Daddy and I will have the spare room, Wendy can share your room, Jean, and the boys can have Angus's room and Angus, you can sleep in the summer house."

"But it leaks," yelled Angus. "Haven't you noticed, the deck chairs are all wet?"

"I'll have to patch it up then," replied Mummy.

"And what about food, Mummy?" I asked. "You've no idea how much they eat. You'll be ruined."

I wanted to see them; but the preparations were spoiling everything. Mummy insisted that all the chair covers had to be washed as well as the bed covers. Angus and I shampooed the carpets; then we polished the brass and suddenly it was Tuesday and I had hardly schooled Phantom at all.

I failed the geometry exam completely. I got twenty out of a hundred for maths, and forty for French. The weather changed and there were days of endless rain and I imagined the Millers, enormous in mackintoshes, saying, "Your crabby English weather!"

Daddy raged about our exam results and threatened us with a cramming school, and Angus said that since he had only passed in English and Geography, he had better be a dustman. Then Daddy hired someone to coach us in the holidays and I imagined the Millers peering over our shoulders while a bearded coach said, "Recite the verb to sit in the imparfait."

Angus was very bad-tempered. He said there was no point in living if we were going to be coached all through the summer holidays and that he was going to commit suicide while the Millers were staying so that everyone in the world would know what awful lives English children lived. "It's nothing but education from the cradle till middle age," he shouted.

The orchard was soaking wet and so was the paddock and there was hardly any time to ride. Daddy saw the headmaster and we were given extra homework and still it rained. I wondered what I could sell to pay Mr. Miller when Phantom refused to enter the ring. I had two cups which I had won on Moonlight, but neither was silver so they were not worth much. I had some books and a necklace my godmother had left me. It was made of opals and I decided to sell that.

We knew that the Millers were already on their way now, and Angus started to complain about the sheets. "They have super linen ones, different colours for each room," he said.

"And gallons of ice cream," I said. "They can't live without ice cream, Mummy, and saying, 'Hi, what about a coke?' And they don't like orange squash, only orange juice," I added.

Mummy was as nervous as we were. She ordered a turkey and a whole leg of ham and she found tins of cold iced tea in the supermarket, with everything in it but the ice.

The last few days passed far too fast. We started to count blankets and sheets. Then Mermaid developed laminitis and would not move at all and for an awful three hours until the vet came we thought she had something else and would have to be put down. After that Angus spent every spare moment walking her up and down and she had to be kept in the stable and mucked out every morning before school. Finally we both had a Chemistry exam. I could only answer three questions out of twenty-two, but Angus managed eight.

Then Daddy suggested we took the Millers to play tennis on the village courts and we rushed into Henley and bought three more racquets, because mine had decayed while we were in Virginia. And then all too soon it was the day before the Millers' arrival, and we moved Angus's bed into the summer house and tried to patch the roof in vain.

Daddy had had the car washed and serviced by this time and had bought vast quantities of whisky, Dubonnet and cokes. The house looked spotless, more like a hotel I thought than a house where people actually lived. Term had ended but the thought of our tutor hovering over us during lovely summer mornings saying, "How can E equal C, when D doesn't equal B?" hung over us like a huge black shadow.

Chapter Eleven

The telephone was ringing. Daddy was mowing the lawn. Mummy had gone to the village shop to buy some butter.

"You get it," said Angus. "I've got to dig some potatoes for lunch."

I ran into the hall and picked up the receiver, and a voice said, "Hi there. It's Wendy. We've arrived. We're in Reading."

"In Reading!" I exclaimed. "All ready?"

"Sure. Didn't you read the newspapers this morning? We docked early."

"We'll come and fetch you. We'll be there in about forty minutes allowing for traffic hold-ups," I said, wondering if there would be enough lunch for them all.

"Don't be nuts," cried Wendy. "Daddy's getting a cab for us right now. I say, isn't your little island cute? I love your hedges but there's more barbed wire than we've got back home."

"Sure," I answered.

"Here's Pete," Wendy said. There was a sound of giggling and Pete took over. "Hi ya, Jean," he said, "we sure like it over here; it's some place. Here's the old man with a cab, be seeing you."

I put down the receiver and rushed outside. "They've come," I yelled. "They are on their way. Where's Mummy?"

Daddy had stopped mowing the lawn. "Are they at Southampton?" he asked calmly.

"No, Reading!" I cried. "They are on their way in a taxi."

"How super!" cried Angus. "I shall be able to stop thinking about education for a whole week. I'll dig some more potatoes. Who did you talk to?"

"Wendy and Pete. They seem to like our crabby little island," I replied. "I think I'd better put hot water bottles in all the beds; they are sure to find English beds damp."

"Keep calm," Daddy said. "Don't panic. I'll get out the drinks and some ice. Is there enough lunch?"

"I don't know till Mummy's back," I shouted.

"Why are you shouting?" asked Daddy. "It's not very lady-like."

The rain had stopped. A wind blew the trees. It was a typical summer day in England.

I started to scrape potatoes; then Mummy came back.

"I hear they are on their way, and there's only stewed beef and ice cream," she said.

"I've dug some more potatoes," Angus said coming in, his hands covered with earth. "I don't know why you're fussing. Can't we just have hot dogs and cider? I don't think they've tasted cider before. Has anyone got four bob, I'll go and get some."

We were still one chair short in the kitchen, but I didn't mention it. Angus disappeared in search of cider. I finished scraping potatoes. Mummy added some chopped-up bacon to the stew. Daddy was washing his hands upstairs. He had a week's leave from work and had spent the last few days doing what he called "Putting the garden straight."

Mermaid was still in the stable with laminitis. We had hung our few rosettes in the saddle room and cleaned all the tack. I was wearing jeans and an aertex shirt. Mummy wanted me to change. "They won't be in jeans," she said.

"They usually are, and they are not relations," I answered, "and they are used to me in jeans. Honestly, Mummy, must I dress up for the Millers?"

"Oh all right. But I'm going to change," she said. "Watch the potatoes."

"They are coming through the village now," yelled Angus with a bottle of cider in each hand. "I saw the taxi."

"You welcome them. I'm still changing," shouted Mummy.

I rushed down the garden path as they were climbing out of a taxi. "Hiya," I yelled. "Nice to see you."

They looked enormous.

"Heavenly day! Isn't it cute?" cried Mrs. Miller. "But are you sure you can fit us all in, Jean?"

"Where's Phil?" I asked.

"He went on up to London. He's got a girl up there. He's staying with her family. You know Phil," replied Wendy laughing.

"How's the wild horse? You made it then?" asked Mr. Miller.

Daddy had appeared now. "Come and have something to drink, Charlie," he said. "I expect the kids want to see the ponies."

"We're not kids," I said, "not any more. Do you want to see Mermaid and Moonlight and Phantom?" I asked. "There's a show the day after tomorrow. I'm taking Phantom."

"It's all so green," Pete said.

"You didn't crash in the ocean then?" Wendy asked. "It's been kinda quiet back home without you."

.   .   .   .   .   .

Daddy whispered F.H.B. before lunch, which meant family hold back, so Angus and I

110

were not to ask for second helpings. Mr. and Mrs. Miller admired everything. They said that the cottage was full of antiques and that they would sure like to take the whole lot back to Virginia with them. Wendy said that the cottage would be great as a guest house.

They looked too large for the dining room, which had been built five hundred years ago when humans were several inches smaller than us, much less the Millers.

In the afternoon we played clock golf on the lawn and talked. Mummy cooked an enormous dinner and Daddy opened two bottles of wine and we all got rather silly. Mr. Miller kept talking about Phantom. "If you get that horse into a ring day after tomorrow, I'll sure give you five hundred dollars, but if you don't, I sure expect the same from you. That's how I remember it. Am I right?" he asked.

"Yes," I said.

Mummy looked rather pale suddenly. And Daddy said, "Let's have coffee next door, shall we?" and stood up. He shot a piercing glance at me, and I realised that this was the first time he had heard of the bet. I mouthed "Opals," at him but he simply shrugged his shoulders and shepherded the Millers into the sitting room.

I put the kettle on for the coffee and Pete said, "Don't worry, Jean. I'll pay it. I'm loaded with dollars."

And I heard myself reply in rather a haughty voice, "I always pay my debts and I wouldn't dream of borrowing from you. I've got some jewellery," and all the time I was feeling colder and colder and wishing that I had spent more time schooling Phantom rather than shampooing carpets and painting ceilings.

Wendy and I talked for hours that night. The next day they planned to go to Stratford in a hired car. They wanted us to go too, but in the end only Angus went, because I had to spend the day getting Phantom ready for the show. Miss Mackintosh had rung up and we were to leave the riding school at half past eight next morning. Wendy and Pete had promised to help but neither of them could plait a mane, since they had a man at home called Joe who always prepared their horses for shows.

Presently the Millers left in their hired car. It was a large estate and Daddy suddenly decided to go as well as Angus to show them the way.

I helped Mummy with the washing up and she said that she thought they were enjoying themselves all right and that after Saturday they were going back to London and then to visit long-lost relations in Ireland. "But why did you agree to that silly bet with Mr. Miller?" she asked, drying a plate. "You know we can't afford five hundred dollars. You must be mad; it's more than a hundred pounds. I can't think what he's thinking of either."

"I'm going to sell my opals," I answered.

"What, on a Sunday morning? Anyway you shouldn't. Your godmother wouldn't have liked it."

"There's nothing else I can do; besides of course, to win," I added quickly.

"You had better," said Mummy making a face at me.

I caught Phantom and schooled him. I concentrated on making him more obedient to my legs. I did turns on the forehand, half passes and turns on the haunches. Then I did a full pass at the trot and with rising spirits I thought, he's got the makings of a dressage horse. I shall be able to ride him in horse trials. I rode him out of the orchard gate and down the road and turned right towards the riding school, and here the grass and nettles on the verges nearly met across the narrow road. It was a damp English summer morning with the hay cut and carried and the crops of oats and wheat and barley still green in the fields. Small boys were riding an assortment of bikes up and down the road. They shouted, "Ride him, cowboy," and I remembered how Angus had been like that once, small and grubby and mad on his bike, saying a hundred times a day, "Can I go out on my bike? Please, Mummy." And I even then, tangle-haired, small, constantly in dew-drenched plimsolls, could think of nothing but riding.

The riding school was full of pupils when I reached it. "There's no one in the jumping paddock. Try your luck," said Miss Mackintosh. "But don't jump more than a dozen jumps or you'll make him stale."

I rode Phantom round a three foot course and he jumped it easily, only touching one pole which didn't fall. I had entered for the sixteen and under class which was open.

"See you tomorrow at eight thirty. Don't be late," called Miss Mackintosh as I left, pushing her way through a crowd of pupils.

I felt old now. It seemed years since I had been a small child treating Miss Mackintosh as a sort of god. I let Phantom walk home on a loose rein and he ignored the cars which passed and I thought, that's one battle completely won. I put him in Mermaid's loose-box, which is built of brick and flint, but more flint than brick, and I thought, we'll have to find homes for Moonlight and Mermaid. It isn't fair to keep them when we never ride them.

I found Mummy washing lettuce in the sink.

"We're only having a light lunch," she said, and then, "How did he go?"

"Like a dream," I said. "He's too marvellous to be real. But I feel awful about it, because Angus can't ride at all. I think we'll have to sell Moonlight and Mermaid and buy him something."

"They would be lovely to breed from," Mummy answered. "Miss Croft has got an Arab stallion and the fee is quite small, and Mr. Pratt says we can rent his field."

I imagined two foals cantering about the orchard on long legs. "It's just an idea," Mummy said.

"A fabulous one," I cried. "Absolutely fantastic." But it still didn't solve Angus's problem of having no horse to ride.

I spent the afternoon washing Phantom's tail, grooming him until, had he been a piece of furniture, I would have been able to see my face in him. Then I put my grooming things ready in Mummy's shopping basket for the next morning and started on my tack and all the time, I could feel panic growing inside me. I saw Phantom standing on his hind legs, spinning round as he had in Virginia, galloping away, myself just a passenger again. I had decided to put his drop noseband a hole tighter, but it would not stop him rearing. I saw myself abjectly saying, "I'm so sorry I can't pay you yet. But I can on Monday. I've got to sell my opals."

And Mr. Miller would say, "Forget it. It sure doesn't matter." And he would go home to Virginia saying that English people didn't pay their debts, no siree. And I would have sullied my country's name.

I'll say I've got the money in my post office account, I decided and then I started to wonder for the first time how much my opals were worth.

But now the Millers were coming back, laughing as they came up the garden path. "Gee, it was great," Wendy cried. "I sure wanted to be hunting across Warwickshire; those hedges are something. How do they grow so straight?"

I put my girth on top of my saddle. It still needed whitening, but that would have to wait till later. Pete came straight round to the saddle room. "I sure wished you had come," he said. "Do you need any help? I've got a pair of strong arms."

"No, thanks all the same," I said. "Did you have a good time?"

"Sure, it was great," he said, putting an arm on my shoulder. "But I guess you had a miserable time worrying about that silly bet with the old man, huh?"

I nodded slowly.

"And I reckon your opals are not worth more than two hundred dollars. I inquired at a shop in Stratford; not unless they are a double row."

I shook my head.

"Why don't you call the whole thing off?" he suggested. "The old man expects you to. But he won't make the first move."

I saw myself saying, "I agree with what you said, I don't think Phantom will ever go into a ring, here or in Virginia, so please can we call off our bet?" I imagined him holding out his hand, saying, "Now you're talking sense, Jean." And the whole scene was so completely foreign to my nature that I felt like shouting, "No, no, no, I would rather die." But I didn't. I shrugged my shoulders and said, "I'm going to win it. You're all in for a surprise."

Then I hastily touched wood and Pete saw me and said, "You've thought that before. You were real certain you were going to show everyone back home. Be smart, quit now while you've got the chance. No one will despise you for it, no siree."

Suddenly I was hating him for not believing me. "I don't want to talk about it any more," I cried, walking towards the cottage. "If I can't pay, Daddy will have to. We'll sell the family silver, we have our pride."

"A real silly word, pride," shouted Pete. "And where's the silver? I haven't seen any."

My eyes were suddenly brimming with tears because again he didn't believe me. "Turn the spoons over and look," I yelled. "They're worth at least eight pounds each and there are twelve of them—and then there are the forks." We're quarrelling, I thought, and it's never happened before.

Everything had suddenly turned sour. I could hardly speak a word throughout dinner, and the food nearly choked me. I kept looking at Pete and thinking, you traitor! How could you have said such foul things?

Once I caught him looking at the handle of a teaspoon and he blushed.

Angus seemed weary too and soon retired to the summerhouse. It was raining and I was unable to amuse Wendy, for now I could think of nothing but tomorrow.

Finally the Millers decided to watch television with Mummy and Daddy and I wandered to bed feeling a failure in more ways than one. I swallowed three aspirins before climbing into bed and pretended to be asleep when Wendy appeared, muttering, "Crabby English weather."

The words Pete had said, "Where's the silver? I haven't seen any," echoed over and over in my brain. They were stupid enough words, but I felt they were weighted with everything he thought about us, and it was like a sledgehammer hitting some tender spot in my brain again and again.

Chapter Twelve

The weather was fine when I climbed out of bed at five o'clock, dressing quietly so as not to wake Wendy, stopping to pray for one brief moment that Phantom would enter the ring and not let me down. Outside the sun was rising above the elms. Phantom was lying down, looking like a prince, with Mermaid watching over him.

He let me put on a headcollar before he stood up and shook himself. Cocks were crowing everywhere and there was a continuous chorus of birdsong from the trees. The grass was still wet and my jeans were soaked up to the knee by the time I had reached the stable. Outside the road was empty. The whole countryside at this moment seemed to belong to me and the birds and, of course, Phantom.

At seven o'clock I was eating breakfast in the kitchen. Phantom was plaited by this time. When I was struggling into my jodhpur boots Angus appeared from the summerhouse looking sleepy in his pyjamas with a cobweb in his hair.

"Do you want any help? Have you got everything? Don't let us down. You know your opals are probably only worth about fifty pounds," he said.

"I know, I've been told," I answered.

Riding along the road towards the riding school I felt panic coming back. I must think of something else, of school, of Angus's O Levels, of Mermaid in foal; but I couldn't. I could only imagine Mr. Miller waiting for his money. The post van was coming down the road now and I could see cows being turned into a meadow after milking. Phantom was carrying himself marvellously. I felt as though we were trotting on air.

The trailer was waiting in the yard, its ramp down, when I reached the riding school. Miss Mackintosh appeared in breeches and boots, white shirt, tie and hairnet. "It's going to be a glorious day," she said. "I'll load mine first."

She led out a big chestnut with two white socks behind. I wondered how she mounted so big a horse, as she led him towards the trailer. Three minutes later I was leading Phantom up the ramp, talking to him, saying, "This is our great day. You must behave."

Miss Mackintosh put the ramp up. "So far, so good," she said. "I'll just get my hat and coat and then we're off."

"Mummy and Daddy are bringing oats and grooming things," I said, putting my saddle and bridle in Miss Mackintosh's Landrover.

I sat in the front. The journey took an hour or more and was uneventful, except that I had a pain now in my right side and my legs had started to feel like jelly.

The show was in a stadium; there were no green

trees, no open space. Only the trains tearing along a track fifty yards away, and tarmac, and dusty earth and cars. "No one told me it was here," I cried. "Phantom will never go in. He will think it's a trap. Why didn't someone tell me it was in a stadium?"

"It was on the schedule," replied Miss Mackintosh.

"It must have been in jolly small letters then," I said.

"Keep calm and he'll keep calm," suggested Miss Mackintosh. She was riding her chestnut in the Novice Jumping for Grade C horses. I left Phantom in the trailer and watched the hacks being judged. The sun was shining and there were only a few people in the tiers of seats round the stadium. After a time I unboxed Phantom and tied him to the outside of the trailer and polished him with the stable rubber. I was feeling sick now. I simply couldn't imagine Phantom going into the stadium. I tacked up and walked him up and down, letting him look at everything. My class was at ten-thirty and the fourteen and under jumping was in progress.

I had never ridden in so large a show before. I cursed myself for entering without reading the front of the schedule and found myself longing for the small, cosy gymkhanas at which I had competed so often on Moonlight; where the first prize was ten shillings and everyone knew everyone else.

But now my parents and Angus and the Millers had arrived. "Some show," shouted Wendy.

"Phantom looks great, and so do you," called Pete, no doubt trying to make up for the unpleasantness of the evening before. They looked very American, and I think quite a few people immediately decided I was American too.

"If you think Phantom's going in that stadium you're even nuttier than I ever imagined," Mr. Miller told me.

I shrugged my shoulders. Secretly I agreed with him—it seemed impossible that Phantom would ever canter round the green turf with the people watching on all sides—but I wasn't going to let Mr. Miller know. I was determined to keep pretence up till the last minute of defeat.

Daddy was wearing cotton trousers and a checked shirt. He patted Phantom and said quietly, "Don't let us down, Jean. Ride as though our lives depended on it."

The pain seemed to be growing in my side now and the winner of the fourteen and under jumping was coming out of the ring with a cup in her hand. If only it was over, I thought, if only I could go home and bury my head in some sand and never see the Millers again.

Pete pulled up my girths. "You were sure right about the spoons," he said. "You've got plenty and they're all silver."

But now the spoons didn't matter any more. The whole of the evening before was trivial compared with what was going on in the ring, for now men were putting up the jumps. There were eleven of them and they were going up to three foot six at least.

"You look a bit green," said Angus glancing at me with a nervous smile lurking behind his eyes. "Shall I lead him up to the entrance when the moment comes?"

"If you like." I was feeling indifferent, somehow removed from it all now. I think that I simply couldn't face the suspense any more and had temporarily switched some part of myself off.

"They are calling you into the collecting ring," Mummy told me. "All the luck in the world . . ."

She was wearing a suit and sling-back shoes.

"The same from here," cried Mrs. Miller. "And don't you go worrying about Charlie's bet. Heavenly day, we don't expect you to pay five hundred dollars."

"I won't pay because I'm going in. But otherwise, I always pay my debts."

Brave words! They seemed to come from a long way off. It wasn't really me speaking, but someone else, some ancestor braver than myself speaking for me.

I told the collecting-ring steward my number. It was thirteen.

"Thirteen!" shouted Wendy. "Gee whizz!"

Angus held Phantom while I walked the course. Surveying the jumps I felt sicker every second. There was a terrible combination of three, an enormous wall, a spread of parallel bars which seemed wider than any jump I had ever imagined and finally, a water jump. If it wasn't for the five hundred dollars I would be happy to remain outside, I thought, mounting again.

"Some jumps," Wendy said. "They sure look big— like Madison Square Garden."

I started to talk to Phantom. "We are going in there," I said. "It isn't a corral, there's nothing to worry about. Look, ponies are going in and coming out without any trouble; there's nothing to it." People were looking at me now but I ignored them. Phantom cocked an ear back and listened. I can't remember all

121

Phantom jumping at the show

I said, I just continued in the same voice, talking and stroking his neck.

Angus pulled off his tail bandage. "You're next," he said. "Good luck."

The collecting steward said, "Ready? All right, go in, but wait for the bell."

I could see the crowd in tiers of seats round the ring. Mr. Miller was out there somewhere watching, so were Mummy and Daddy. Phantom was walking forward now, calmly, his neck arched. He played with his bit and dropped his nose and suddenly we were in the ring, trotting round waiting for the bell, and all my fear had gone, to be replaced by a feeling of immense confidence.

I prayed for the bell to ring soon and it did. I closed my legs against Phantom's sides and we were cantering towards the first jump. Phantom slowed down and for one terrible moment I thought, he's going to refuse, and it was something he had never done before. Then it was behind us and we were cantering towards the next fence, a road-closed sign, and now he was taking over. He didn't hesitate. In mid-air he seemed to kick his hind legs even higher and then we were racing on towards the parallel bars. After that came the wall, the gate, the fearsome combination where he took off too early for the last fence and scraped the top and there was an "Oh" from the crowd, but it didn't fall. There were crossbars and a stile and another jump I hardly noticed, then there was only one more jump now before the water. I slowed him down a little and then we were over that too, racing towards the water and I thought, don't let go yet, Jean, you're nearly clear, steady, steady, and then we were over and from the stands came a tremendous burst of clapping and I fell forward on Phantom's neck, patting him and saying over and over again, "We've done it."

"You're the only clear round so far," cried Angus, rushing to meet me.

"It was great," cried Pete. "You've won the bet."

"Doggone it, as if she doesn't know," cried Wendy.

A voice quite near said, "They're Americans. They must have come over especially. I bet she ends up jumping for the United States."

"Actually I'm English," I said turning round. "These are my friends from America. If I jump for any country it will be England."

They looked embarrassed.

"There's a jump off," Daddy said. "Well done, Jean."

Mr. Miller held out an envelope. "It's yours, Jean," he told me. "You've sure earned it."

I didn't know what to say. At last I managed, "It's too much. You've done so much for us already."

"Exactly," agreed Daddy trying to push away his hand.

"I pay my debts," replied Mr. Miller. "This girl was prepared to sell the family silver and her jewellery for hers. I sure don't have to."

"Please don't, Charlie," pleaded Mummy.

"Take it, Jean," shouted Mr. Miller, pushing it into my hand. "And don't ever let it be said that Virginians don't pay their gambling losses."

"They are putting up the jumps," Angus said. "You'll be going first in the jump off."

I rode in with the five hundred dollars in my pocket. Phantom danced a little and looked at the crowds, as though this time he knew they were there watching him. Then the bell sounded and we were cantering towards the first fence and as he jumped I suddenly knew what I would spend the dollars on—a horse for Angus who was standing now in the wings watching, a stable rubber in his hand. Phantom knocked the next fence, probably because my mind wasn't with him, for at that moment I was seeing a new horse coming to live at Sparrow Cottage.

The course was six inches higher except for the water jump which remained the same, but I didn't notice it. We went faster this time and Phantom raced over the combination with a tremendous flourish as if to make up for rapping a fence last time. And now again we were racing for the water, and I sensed the tenseness of the crowd, the sudden hushed silence, which was quiet enough to let me hear the drone of an aeroplane overhead. Phantom took off too early, but it didn't matter for he had no intention of getting his hoofs wet. There was a burst of applause and I knew we were clear. I put my reins in one hand and cantering out, I could hear a train and Angus yelling, "Well done."

This time Miss Mackintosh was there to greet me too.

"What an achievement!" she cried. "Well done, Jean."

I leapt off to find oats in my pockets for Phantom. The other clear round was going in now—a boy on a chestnut as lean as himself.

"Don't hurry him, let him look," said his mother, small and plump in dark glasses.

"It was a pity you hit the second fence," said Miss Mackintosh. "What happened?"

I remembered that she had always been keen on

post-mortems. "I was thinking of something else," I said.

She made a tut-tutting noise.

The sun was shining on us all now and I longed to take off my coat. We could not see the whole ring, but someone said, "He's over the first three clear."

Angus started twisting the stable rubber into knots and biting his nails. A voice said, "Is your horse for sale? Because if he is, I would like to make an offer."

I shook my head and turned to see a military-looking man running his sharp eyes over Phantom. "I'll give you six hundred."

"He's not for sale. I'm keeping him forever," I said.

"He's hit the combination, he's stopped, the boy's falling off," shouted Angus. "You've won."

The Millers were running down the steps from the stands. The boy was coming out leading his chestnut. Angus was jumping up and down. "Number Twenty-five has been eliminated," announced the loudspeaker.

Angus pulled up my girths. Daddy started stroking Phantom's neck. Mummy said, "You've won."

Pete said, "Holy smoke! I never knew he could jump like that. You wait till I tell them back home."

"They won't believe you," I replied, suddenly seeing the valley again in my imagination—the parched earth, the mountains in the distance, the Millers' house, the people saying, "Sure, but we don't believe you. That little horse will never make good, no siree."

"Oh yes they will," answered Pete. "I've got it all here real good. I brought a roll of film. I'll be sending

126

it to the newspapers. I'll let the whole of Virginia know."

I wanted to say, "You're fantastic," but at that moment the loudspeaker announced, "Will the following numbers come into the ring: Number Thirteen. Miss Jean Simpson on Phantom . . ." I was riding in now and somewhere a band was playing. Phantom danced and tossed his head and I kept remembering the first time I had seen him galloping wild and alone across the moonlit valley. It all seemed to have happened years ago. I halted in the centre of the ring and the boy on the chestnut stopped beside me, and the band was still playing and the sun still shining and it was one of those golden moments which you never forget.

Everything seemed possible now, jumping for England, riding at Madison Square Garden in New York, doing the American circuit, all the big shows in the United States, and Canada—Toronto, Montreal. And now we were cantering round and I could see the Millers and Mummy and Daddy and Angus waiting outside, and nothing mattered now but the feel of the turf beneath us and Phantom's effortless canter which felt as though it could last for ever, through countless rings, round Badminton, through days and days of hunting, for half my life at least.

by Christine Pullein-Thompson

PHANTOM HORSE

"I gazed in wonder at the view. Suddenly I saw something moving at great speed below us. It was a horse galloping riderless and alone. He moved beautifully and with tremendous grace. His tail streamed behind him like a pennant. He looked like something out of another world. It was the wild Palomino . . ."

The thrilling story of how Angus and Jean take Phantom from the wild Blue Ridge Mountains of America and make him their own.

PHANTOM HORSE GOES TO IRELAND

"Phantom was lying on his side, kicking against the partition, making a terrible noise. He was soaked in sweat. His tattered mane clung to his neck and his sides were spattered with peat.

Angus hit him, saying, 'Phantom, get up. Come on, move.'

All the time my heart was beating like a piston engine and I was imagining the end – Phantom dead . . ."

Phantom helps his owners solve an exciting mystery – but will it be at the expense of his own life?

PHANTOM HORSE IN DANGER

"We know that Craig is buying horses under false pretences," Dominic continued. "Not for good homes, but for slaughter. We need proof. I am going to sell him Phantom as a stolen horse – and then alert the police. Don't worry, Jean. We'll get him back again, I promise."

But the plan to trap the cruel horse dealer goes horribly wrong. Terror-struck, Jean and Angus realise they may never see Phantom alive again.

Armada